To Jeon
Enjoy the read

CAPITAL MURDER

BY: RICK STIENS

Rick Stiens

Capital Murder is a work of fiction. Names, characters, places, and incidents either are the products of the author's imagination or are used fictitiously. Any resemblance to actual events, locales or persons, living or dead, is entirely coincidental.

Copyright © 2005 by Rick Stiens

ISBN #978-0915-725 11-8

In memory of my parents
Oliver & Rita Stiens

Acknowledgments

When I started writing this book I had no idea how many people would give their time, their talent and their energy to make this work. I thank all of you from the bottom of my heart for making my dream become a reality.

To everyone who critiqued the novel and gave me their suggestions and encouragement, thank you.

To Simon Anderson, my mentor and friend, whose wisdom and guidance over the past four years challenged me to become the best writer I could.

To Michael Banks, an incredibly talented writer and editor, who helped mold and shape the story into the form it is today. It would not have worked without him.

To Judy Stiens and Angel Joseph, whose edits, input and insights were critical to the improvement of the novel. They got me over the last hurdle.

To Peter Bronson, for all his help, suggestions and advice along the road to publication.

To my daughter Marissa, for designing the art work for the cover. Somehow she was able to translate a half baked, sketchy idea I had in my head into a book jacket that was off the charts.

To my daughters Liz and Sallie, and my son Rick and his wife Jen, thank you for your love, encouragement and support.

Last, but certainly not least, my greatest debt goes to my loving wife Donna. She has been my in house editor, creative consultant and the person who has been there from day one. From the original manuscript, through every rewrite she has counseled me, nudged me, and helped make sense of it all. This book is as much hers as it is mine. She never doubted, nor would she let me, that writing this novel would be a great experience. She shared my dream and made it happen for us.

Chapter One

WASHINGTON, D.C. - TUESDAY 9:00 PM

"Belinda, you look absolutely stunning tonight," John Harrington said easing her dress up and caressing the inside of her thigh. He steered the Cadillac Escalade along the narrow roadway into the Rock Creek parking area, near a thick stand of trees.

"You are such a sweetheart Senator," she purred in her sexy southern drawl. "You're the reason I look so special tonight. I could never have afforded this dress. It's the nicest gift you've ever given me. I knew when I saw that black crepe, deep-front cut at Bloomingdale's the other day it would be the perfect formal gown to wear to the party tonight."

"The Israeli Embassy hasn't seen a guest like you in a long time. That's why we had a steady stream of people coming over all night to talk to us. Everybody wanted to meet you. You were the belle of the ball. You got it all babe — brains, looks, personality."

"You're too sweet."

As the car rolled into the parking lot his headlights picked out a dark colored Honda Accord, a Georgetown University sticker on the bumper. He laughed and slid his hand higher on her leg as he angled the car to the opposite end of the dark parking lot, away from the light pole near the entrance. He nodded toward the Honda, "Vestiges of my misspent youth. These kids are smart. They know where to go when they need some privacy."

"Is this where you brought your girlfriends when you went to Georgetown?" she chided him.

"Guilty as charged," the senator replied as he nudged the car into the last parking space.

Belinda laid her head back against the seat, immersed in the moment. A combination of alcohol and skin-to-skin contact made her skin flush. After he turned off the ignition and released his seatbelt Harrington kissed Belinda on the lips, and began to pull the spaghetti straps off her shoulders. He slipped the dress down to her waist and kissed her neck, sliding down until he reached her breasts. She purred at him and grabbed his head with both hands, pulling him closer to her body.

He stopped for a moment and reached across her leg to press the seat adjustment button. The leather seat slid back and reclined at the same time. After a long wet kiss John Harrington pulled away and plopped back down into the driver's seat.

With the moonlight shining through her window, Belinda looked over at him as she pulled off her four-inch heels and squirmed out of her dress. Wearing only her black, thigh-high stockings and the jewelry that he had given her, she ran her tongue around the outside of her lips.

"Hang on baby, I'll be there in a flash," Harrington promised.

The senator tossed his coat on the back seat, kicked off his shoes, un-buckled his belt, and slid his slacks and boxer shorts down. Twenty seconds later he was lying on top of her. Her smooth, silky body welcomed him inside.

When their lovemaking was over, Harrington rolled his head to the side of hers. They lay together, spent, taking short, hard breaths, making no effort to move. Her arms were extended around his back, his head resting against her breasts.

"I'm the luckiest guy in the world," he proclaimed.

Their last sigh was followed by an explosion of glass that shattered across their bodies. The car alarm blared. Belinda screamed as the senator's blood spattered her face. Four soft pings in quick succession were followed by a couple more. Neither of the blood soaked bodies moved after the last shot.

The killer ran around to the driver's side and smashed the window with the butt of his gun. He pulled the keys from the ignition and pressed the key pad. The doors unlocked and the alarm stopped. Harrington's cell phone rang.

The killer ignored it and grabbed the senator's wallet and Belinda's purse off the back seat. He sprinted through the woods that bordered the parking lot to get back to his car. After he ripped off his ski mask and gloves he jumped behind the wheel of the Honda. He shoved the mask, gloves, wallet and purse in a black trash bag, along with a five-pound bag of sugar. He wrapped the top of the trash bag with duct tape several times and slid it under his black windbreaker, next to the gun.

The Honda shot out of the parking lot and the killer adjusted his Georgetown baseball cap with the bill facing backward. After driving faster than he should have for about ten minutes, he reached Nebraska Avenue and slowed down. A few minutes later he made a left on Wisconsin and drove at a steady twenty-five miles per hour through Georgetown to avoid getting pulled over by a cop. When he reached M Street, the sidewalks were crowded and there was a steady stream of cars. His anxiety level began to drop.

Half a block from the Key Bridge, traffic came to a halt. All he could see up ahead in his lane were blue and red flashing lights. Traffic was light headed his way and he debated making a U turn, but the cars in front of him started to move again. He saw a cop with a flashlight motioning cars to go around him. When he got a little closer to the action the killer breathed a sigh of relief. A metro tow truck driver was putting the hook underneath a dark blue compact parked in a red tow zone.

After nodding his head and waving to the cop, he pulled back into the curb lane and made a right onto the Key Bridge. He wound down the passenger side window and looked in the rearview mirror. When the bridge was clear of oncoming traffic, he slowed down and threw the gun into the river. Then he tossed the plastic bag after it and sped up until he reached the sign for the Best Western Hotel on the other side of the bridge.

He pulled into the hotel's ground level parking area, looking for empty spaces toward the rear where the lighting was dim. As he approached the rear wall he spotted a space between it and an extended cargo van. Perfect. The shooter eased into the space.

He wiped the steering wheel and door handles with his jacket and headed down the exit ramp to the sidewalk in front of the hotel. Several cars passed before he was able to cross the street and walk south to the subway tunnel.

Three minutes later he was standing at the Roslyn subway entrance. He looked around while he stood in line behind a half-dozen people waiting to take the escalator down to the train platform. When he got to the bottom of the escalator he hopped off, slid his card in and passed through the gate.

The trip to the National Mall was quick and uneventful, as was the cab ride over to Reagan Airport. The route wasn't direct, but was necessary to cover his tracks. An hour later he was on his way back to Miami, sipping on a rum and Coke, looking down at the Capitol from his seat in first class.

Chapter Two

_____

ROCK CREEK PARK, WASHINGTON, D.C.
10:15 PM

By the time Charlie Brune got to the crime scene, the forensic team from the District had isolated the area. The parking lot was cordoned off with yellow tape and the night lights were up and running.

After he flashed his Justice Department ID to the officer at the parking lot entrance, he was allowed to pass through and park his car. The first person he recognized was the sandy haired and stocky built District homicide investigator Russell Trupp. Brune had worked with him in the past and found him to be a first-rate investigator. He had tried unsuccessfully to lure him over to DOJ to work for him full time.

"It didn't take you long to get here," Trupp noted as he extended his hand toward Brune.

"Your liaison office caught me on my cell just as I pulled into my driveway. I live in Chevy Chase, not too far from here," Brune answered as he shook hands with him.

"Excuse me a minute," Trupp said, as he turned to one of the uniforms present, "Officer Linck take another officer with you and block off the entry road before the rest of the press gets here. I don't want to give them or anyone else a chance to contaminate the crime scene. After the remainder of the DC press corps gets here, tell them somebody will be down to give them a briefing."

"Yes, sir," the officer said as he walked toward his squad car.

"Tell me why a U.S. Senator is having sex in the park?" Trupp asked rhetorically as the two men walked toward a bank of lights surrounding the Escalade.

"That's what happened here?" Brune said, taken by surprise.

"I'd say Bubba Harrington either couldn't wait or couldn't risk going to a hotel for fear of being recognized," Brune offered. "So he came here for a quickie. You know how this town thrives on scandal."

"That's as good a guess as any. I assume you want DOJ to have jurisdiction, since a U.S. Senator is one of the victims."

"That would be the case, Russell. Operationally, this will be a joint investigation with Justice as the lead. But in reality it's your case. You'll be the lead investigator and since your forensic people are already here it makes sense to have them process all the physical evidence. Just copy me on that and anything else you turn up. One more thing, it has to be done by computer."

"That works for me. Nothing could please me more. I get the best of both worlds. While I work on the case you get to deal with the Washington press corps and all those assholes up on Capitol Hill."

"Just one of the privileges of rank," Brune said cynically. "I'm going to bring in somebody from my office to help with the investigation. Someone low key to dig into this guy's background. Bubba was a major player on the Hill. I'm sure like all politicians he has some skeletons in his closet and my guy will be able to look where you can't. We'll pursue it from that end and work the case together as a team."

Trupp nodded. "I'll run a check of our database to see if his plates come up with us or the Park Police. Maybe he's been here before, or maybe he was tagged somewhere else that might give us some kind of lead. We keep a record of every ticket issued, and every vehicle stopped within the District is on file in our database."

"Even if the tickets get tossed," Brune asked.

"Yeah, even when the tickets get tossed," Trupp confirmed.

"What about cars with diplomat tags?"

"Especially them. Hell, you can't boot 'em and have them towed for parking illegally like every other resident of the District. So we do the next best thing. Pull their ass over whether they are driving erratically or not. Just to let them know we're keeping an eye on them," Trupp winked at Brune.

"Given the heightened security concerns, we like to know the areas that these people frequent, particularly those with Middle Eastern diplomatic tags. I'll see if any of them have been stopped in or around the park."

"Sounds like profiling to me," the Justice Agent smirked.

"You bet your ass it is."

"I'm impressed," Brune chuckled.

"You ought to be. It was the Anti-Terror Unit at Justice that set the program up."

A surprised look came across Brune's face. "I had no idea. Good plan though."

"Operationally we are going to function on a need-to-know basis I assume," Trupp asked.

"That's the way it has to be, the four of us, which includes your chief of course. It's the only way we can guarantee control. Who knows what we are going to uncover," Brune said as he squinted inside the car.

"I'll start with the senator's family and the house in Silver Springs and see where that leads. I'm betting you're going to start at his congressional office."

"You're right. That's where I plan to be first thing in the morning. I'll talk to you at some point later in the day after we get a secure phone line set up in your office. And while we're at it I'll also get you a secure cell phone for the field."

"That'll be great," Trupp said.

"While my tech support guys are at your office, I'll make sure they set up an encrypted computer system that can interface with mine. That will allow for the secure transfer of information back and forth. On your end keep everything on disc and take it home with you every night. I don't want any paper records."

"Good, that clears up all the security concerns I had," Trupp said.

Brune hesitated for a moment then said, "Any wiretaps or search warrants you might need will have to be executed through my office. I can get them for you in a heartbeat. That should cover all the logistical issues. What about you?"

"I'm good. I think you covered all the bases except money for manpower needs, which I'm sure my chief is going to want at some point," Trupp pointed out.

"Yeah, I figured that, and it won't be an issue. I've got a discretionary budget to handle that when the time comes. Russ, I hope you're able to get some sleep tonight. Tomorrow is going to be a tough first day."

"My forensic guys are going to be here all night, but I'll be out of here in a couple of hours," Trupp said.

"I'll deal with the press on my way out."

"Thanks Charlie. Talk to you in the morning," Trupp said as he headed back to the Escalade.

Chapter Three

SARASOTA, FLORIDA - 10:15 PM

"We'll be touching down in five minutes Mr. Harper," the pilot radioed back from the flight deck.

"Thanks Kevin, I'll buckle up," Martin Harper answered through the speaker on his seat panel.

The Gulfstream V banked gently to the east and began its final approach into Sarasota airport. The pilot picked up the outer marker lights to the west of Highway 41, followed the guide slope crossing the outer perimeter of the airport and landed a couple of minutes later.

The jet taxied across the runway until it reached Jonas Aviation hanger about a half-mile from the main terminal area. When the aircraft stopped a green light flashed at the rear of the cabin. Harper unbuckled his seatbelt, grabbed his briefcase and headed for the exit door located just behind the flight cabin.

The exit door stairway was extending to the ground by the time he got there.

He paused at the doorway. "Another great flight Kevin, you and Paul are the best."

"Thank you sir," both men answered at the same time.

"You guys enjoy your time at the beach. I'll touch base with you during the week and let you know when we're headed out again," he told them as he walked down the stairway to the tarmac.

The door to the hangar was up and his red Z-8 Corvette convertible was sparkling like a shiny gem in the moonlight. He opened the car door, slid down behind the wheel and laid his briefcase on the tan leather seat next to him. After he fastened his seatbelt and adjusted the steering wheel, he turned the ignition key. The high-performance engine poured out the throaty signature sound that Harper liked hearing so well.

"Daddy's home baby," he said as he pushed the CD button.

A soft refrain from Michael Franks' *A Walk In The Rain* began to play as he guided the car onto Tallevast Road. When he got to the merge for Route 41 South he accelerated and shifted into second gear. After he reached fifty miles-per-hour he shifted into fourth gear, then fifth, and eased off the accelerator.

The combination of warm, moist, salty night air and soft jazz welcomed him back like an old friend. Cruising down the palm lined boulevard in his ruby colored 'Vette, the silver haired banker looked over at the signature purple dome of the Van Wezel Performing Center to his right—a place where he had been many times to attend concerts and charity functions.

He took in a deep breath and smiled reflectively. Life had been good to him. He had just left his girlfriend Sherry Novaks in Cincinnati. After a night and day spent at her riverfront condominium, he was home. Back to the other loves of his life: his car, his boat, and his palatial surroundings in Sarasota.

His career path had been a long one, but he had made it to the top as one of Florida's financial, social and political leaders. His roots as a poor South Carolina farm boy, who never had two nickels to rub together while growing up, were a driving force in his life. So were the summers working the fields picking fruit to pay his college tuition.

Both gave him an appreciation for hard, honest work, and the value of money. He had worked long hours, invested wisely and did what was necessary to accumulate the wealth he craved. His entrée into banking began with a job at Citadel S&L after graduation. He moved up the ladder, became president, and later accumulated enough money to buy the family owned business that included four branches. He quickly increased the number of branches to ten and expanded his operations into Florida in part thanks to contacts with wealthy retired Cincinnatians who moved south.

Investments in land, strip malls, and the booming Florida real estate market, with the help of Florida Coastal Bank President Ronnie Gibson, took him to the next level. The two men met at a banking conference at Sawgrass Golf Course some years earlier. Because they shared a similar background, growing up poor and struggling for everything they had, they became good friends.

Appointments to the boards of numerous corporations, including Florida Coastal, gave him access to a broad network of financial resources and investors. Access to the capital markets was the key toward possessing the crown jewel of a lifetime, ownership of a bank. When Gulfcoast Bank went on the block, he was there to scoop it up.

He formed a partnership with Gibson to help secure investment capital for the acquisition. Gibson brought Thomas Vasquez, a long-time customer and friend, into the mix to help finance the deal.

Vasquez was an ex-military man and consular official from Colombia. He had a broad portfolio of real estate holdings, a tile and marble distributorship and an export-import business with locations in Sarasota and Miami. This marriage of convenience between the parties paved the way for Harper to become wealthy, but it came with a hefty price tag, in the form of his dependence on Vasquez.

Thomas Vasquez deposited millions of dollars in cash annually from his various businesses, as did his network of friends. Harper didn't know, or care, in the beginning whether the money was dirty. When the brass ring was within reach, Vasquez made it happen. Harper owed him and he knew it. Keeping a blind eye to the source was the cost of getting the bank.

Harper had cultivated his political relationship with Democratic Party leaders in Florida through his fund raising efforts. He utilized his business contacts in support of that effort and was the largest fundraiser in the state. Politicians at the local and federal level were indebted to him.

He understood early on the relationship between money and politics. When the time was right he stepped up to the plate and delivered huge sums of cash to all the right places, especially Washington. He bought his ambassadorship to Switzerland, a part time ceremonial position, using the time honored tradition of being the largest single contributor to the president's re-election campaign committee. Every move he made had been meticulously calculated.

The banker knew that his money, political connections in Washington, his ambassadorship to Switzerland, virtually everything in his life was dependent on his relationship with Vasquez and Gibson. Vasquez was a major source of business and Gibson, as CEO, was responsible for running the day-to-day operations of the bank.

The firewall that Harper had created was the arms-length relationship that existed on paper between himself and Gibson. He was chairman of the board, but all the legal responsibility rested on Gibson's shoulders, despite the fact that Harper controlled every major decision that was made.

He instituted the separation of powers within the company as an insurance policy. If things went south and there were financial, legal, or regulatory issues with the bank, Gibson was left holding the bag. By insulating himself from the daily operations he had plausible deniability. It would be his word against Gibson's. And it was the CEO Gibson who signed off on all the documents.

By design, there weren't any documents, e-mails, or any other forms of evidence to link Harper to the decision-making process. The only tangible thread of connection was the informal monthly audit and loan committee meetings that all board members attended. It was a glorified dog-and-pony show to satisfy the Feds. Gibson would informally tell the board what he had done, and they would approve it, after the fact.

Harper, Gibson, and Vasquez, along with four other hand-picked members, comprised the bank's board of directors. Together they were the seven largest shareholders, with Harper's twenty percent constituting the largest single holding.

As long as nobody got greedy or stupid, everything would be just fine. By keeping everything on an even keel everyone could continue to make money. Harper was cautious about his relationships with people, never totally trusting anyone. He learned early on, after he got burned on one of his first deals, to abide by the old axiom: Keep your friends close, and your enemies closer. He viewed his relationship with Gibson and Vasquez as falling somewhere in between.

As he prepared to exit the highway he was jarred back to reality by the trilling of his cell phone.

"Hello Martin, this is Thomas. I've got bad news. Bubba Harrington has been shot and killed up in D.C."

Harper sat in stunned silence, then dropped the phone down to his leg. After a couple of seconds he raised it to his ear and said, "Jesus, that's terrible! What the hell happened?"

"I don't know. I just caught a clip of it on the television as I walked by the bar on the way upstairs to the restaurant. How close are you?"

"I'm about five minutes out."

"We'll talk more when you get here."

"You got that right," Harper answered back.

Chapter Four

SARASOTA, FLORIDA - 10:30 PM

Harper stopped the car in the valet parking area at the front of Marina Park Restaurant. A valet walked up to the car, opened his door and handed him a ticket.

"Good to see you again Mr. Harper."

"It's great to be back Ramon," he told the attendant as he put the valet ticket into his pocket.

He hustled into the lobby of the restaurant and was greeted by the manager. "Mr. Vasquez is up at your table waiting for you," he told him.

"Thanks Josh," he answered as he bounded up the circular stairway to the main dining area.

Harper saw the tan, angular body of his associate silhouetted against a table by the window. Vasquez was looking out at the marina and Sarasota Bay off in the distance but turned his head just as he got to the table.

"Thomas, I can't believe somebody killed Bubba Harrington," Harper said as he dropped into the seat across from Vasquez. "He was a U.S. Senator for God's sake. What the hell would be the motive?" Harper asked in an agitated tone.

"Who knows? The information on the television was sketchy, but it did mention another person with him was also killed," Vasquez said.

"I'll tell you who it wasn't. It wasn't some jealous guy and it wasn't his wife. Maybe we'll know more tomorrow," Harper said as a waiter approached the table.

"Good evening Mr. Harper, Mr. Vasquez. Can I get you gentlemen something to drink while you look at tonight's menu?"

"That would be great Phillipe. I'll have a Maker's Mark on the rocks."

"And I'll have a shot of Jose Cuervo straight up," Vasquez told the waiter.

"Thank you gentlemen, I'll be back shortly."

Harper sipped his water, trying to keep his emotions under control. A couple of minutes later the waiter returned with their drinks. As soon as he was out of hearing distance, Harper leaned across the table and said, "Thomas we just lost our protection in Washington. He kept all those bastards in line who wanted to put more legislation on our backs with tighter regulations and more audits."

"It is a tragedy," his partner sighed as he threw down the tequila and sucked on a slice of lemon.

"Tragedy?" Harper railed. "Thomas it's more than a damn tragedy. We're back to square one, my friend." Harper took a gulp of his bourbon.

"Our only other connection is Senator Murphy, head of the Banking Committee," Harper continued. "I know we help fund his 527 campaign committee. But hell, it was Bubba who greased the skids for us with the legislation. All Murphy got was a little cash. That doesn't buy shit in Washington today. It's all about influence. One guy telling another what to do. We don't have that guy anymore. I'd like to kill the bastard that did this."

Vasquez sat passively across the table, looking over occasionally as Harper rambled on, but staring mostly into the menu. When he finished his drink the waiter returned.

"Would you gentlemen like another round?"

"No Phillipe, I think we need to order," Harper said before Vasquez could reply. "What's the special tonight?"

"Almond-crusted grouper, pan-seared with a light Amaretto cream sauce, served with lemon risotto and braised asparagus."

"That's fine with me and I'll have a spinach salad with sweet and sour dressing to start."

"And for you Mr. Vasquez?"

"I'll have the same entrée with a mixed green salad with raspberry vinaigrette dressing and a crab cake for an appetizer. And we'd like a bottle of Elk Cove Pinot Gris with the meal."

"Excellent pairing with your dinners sir. Do you want your appetizer and your salad at the same time?"

"That would be fine," Vasquez said.

The waiter turned and headed toward the kitchen. Harper sat across the table staring in disbelief as the wine steward came to the table. He showed the bottle of wine to Vasquez for his approval. After uncorking the bottle and giving him a sample he poured a glass for Harper. Then he set the bottle on a small dish in the middle of the table and walked away.

"I have to say your behavior surprises me, given the crisis we're embroiled in. You seem nonplused at best," Harper fumed. "I don't even know if I'm going to be able to eat my dinner and you're ordering food and drink like you don't have a care in the world. Or don't you get it? Our safety net is gone! We're already pushing a ton of cash through the bank. If that pending legislation that Bubba was working on doesn't get out of the Ways and Means Committee we're going to have auditors all over us like white on rice."

"Partner you worry too much. We'll just have to make Senator Murphy our new best friend," the Colombian said with an air of confidence.

"That's the point you don't understand Thomas. That was Harrington's deal. He was the guy who spread the money around and held shit over people's heads to keep them in line. All of that changed now that he's dead. He ruled with an iron hand and I'm sure there are plenty of guys waiting in line to take his job. And who knows if we can deal with the new leader? Whatever influence we had is gone."

The waiter set their salads, bread and appetizer down on the table and asked, "Fresh pepper on your salad?"

"Please," Vasquez answered. The waiter twisted the pepper mill a couple of times then looked at Harper. "And you sir?"

Harper shook his head and the waiter left.

The banker sat back in his chair and stared out at the harbor while the Colombian ate his appetizer. He didn't know what bothered him more, Harrington's death or the attitude of his partner. His concentration was broken when Vasquez called his name.

"Martin we need to talk about the reason you came here. Were there any problems in Zurich setting up the new accounts? Anything unusual, anyone suspicious hanging around?"

"No. I went straight from the airport with the cash to the banks and set up the new accounts with both our names on them. Both have offices in Liechtenstein. So you can wire transfer through either place into the accounts in the Caymans and Antigua."

"Anything unusual at the embassy?" Vasquez wanted to know.

"No I met Rollins, the consular chief from State. He told me as far as the rest of the world knows the Swiss government is not about to change the way they run their banking business, especially their secrecy laws. But because of the terror threat they do cooperate with the U.S. government whenever they get a request for monitoring or get specific requests for information. There haven't been any recent requests for financial records of suspected terror cells, nor have there been any from DEA. The consulate finds out last, but we are told because every request is followed by a phone call from the Swiss government. So even when the government tries to circumvent us, like they do on occasion, I find out."

Before Vasquez could speak again their waiter came back to the table. He cleared their salads away and brought the entrees.

As soon as he left and was out of ear shot Vasquez told Harper, "That shouldn't affect us since we have three separate banking houses now. We can take more money over every couple of weeks and spread it around."

Harper ate a bite of his fish and glared across the table. Vasquez looked back.

"That isn't going to happen," Harper said as took another bite of his dinner.

His partner laid his fork down on the plate, and wiped his mouth with the white linen napkin. "What the hell do you mean? That was the main reason we opened the other accounts."

"No Thomas. The main reason we did it was to spread the risk," he said as he reached into his jacket and handed him two navy blue deposit books.

"We now have three banks with three different dummy corporations. All the money I take to

Switzerland goes through in diplomatic pouches and suitcases. I'm not about to start filling up chests with cash. It's risky enough the way it is. My concern isn't the Swiss banking officials, it's the U.S. government agencies. There's no way in hell I'm going to three different banks the same day with diplomatic pouches. The intelligence agencies surely must have operatives that we don't know about monitoring the banks. Increased visibility on my part means increased scrutiny from them. My name comes up for investigation and so does yours. We can't have that."

Vasquez threw his napkin down on the table. Harper continued to eat, then paused between bites to speak again. "You really should finish your meal. The grouper is delicious."

The veins on the Colombian's neck began to bulge.

"Thomas there may be a way to do want you want."

Vasquez put both hands on the table and leaned forward. "Go ahead, I'm listening."

"We may be able to accommodate everyone's interests and still keep the government out of our hair. I'm flying down to the Caribbean next week to open additional accounts. And just like Switzerland I'll be able to use my diplomatic immunity to bring the currency in. By laundering additional currency there along with diamonds we increase the number of banks in our network."

Harper let the Colombian take in what he said for a minute before proceeding. "The downside is that we'll have to move it through more locations and consequently it will take more time. On the flip side though, it spreads the risk out for everybody, especially your business associates in Panama and Columbia."

Vasquez took a drink of his wine and nodded.

"You'll have to talk to your business associates to work out the additional transfer of money and diamonds to us, but I'm sure that won't be a problem," Harper said.

"That's why I like doing business with you, Martin," Vasquez said as he grinned at him. "You're the smartest son-of-a-bitch I ever met."

Chapter Five

CHEVY CHASE, MARYLAND – WEDNESDAY
9:00 AM

Richard Herzog had been weighing a career change for some time. Despite the fact that he liked his job he had the itch to do something different. Something that would get him out from behind a desk. He never dreamed the opportunity would be dropped in his lap by his former CIA boss from Vietnam, Charlie Brune.

Herzog was the chief policy analyst for the Croft Institute, a Washington consulting firm. His company did business with State, the NSC, and other federal agencies. Over the years he had kept in touch with his old boss who was Director of the criminal prosecution division at the Department of Justice.

He met Brune in country after he graduated from the Army sniper school. They worked together in the rural pacification program that the CIA ran in Vietnam. The other part of the job was laying the intelligence groundwork to disrupt the flow of men and materials down the Ho Chi Minh Trail through Cambodia. Early on Herzog worked as a sniper and observer. He was highly efficient at his job, operating with a partner in the field for days at a time.

Based on his reports of activity in the field and troop movements Brune brought him in to work with his team. Herzog became more involved in the rural pacification efforts, working with local villages and winning them over. The intelligence they got from the villages was a critical link in their interdiction efforts.

Coordination of this information with that of reconnaissance patrols in the field gave Brune the broader picture that he needed. The special effort it took, and the quality of information he received from Herzog's work were second to none. Brune's unit became a formidable force which laid the groundwork for successful incursions into Cambodia by larger units.

The reason they were getting together after all these years was a combination of their work history and Brune's desire for an independent, outside investigator. All Herzog knew was that the meeting would be a chance to move on to something different.

He entered the Denny's parking lot and saw his former boss standing beside an older, dark-blue Lincoln. Herzog parked his silver Lexus ES-330 next to Charlie's car.

"Life must be treating you pretty well. You still have a full head of dark hair and no wrinkles on your forehead," Herzog greeted him as he stepped out of his car.

Brune smiled as he looked at his old friend who seemed taller, thinner and grayer than he was the last time they met. "What about you? Nice set of wheels you're driving."

"I'm able to stay up with my bills," Herzog smiled as he shook Brune's hand.

"Thanks for seeing me this morning," he said. "Let's get in my car and I'll explain what's going on."

"That's fine with me," Herzog answered as he sat down in the front seat.

"Where are we headed?"

"Down to the Rayburn Office building, so I can show you what your job is going to be like," Brune said.

"Does our trip down there have anything to do with the murder of John Harrington?"

"It has everything to do with his murder. I'm the head of the joint task force investigating his murder. The guy doing the real work is a fellow from the District named Russell Trupp. I've worked with him before. He's their top investigator. Russell is going to run it on the forensic side and build the case from the physical evidence his crew assembles."

The analyst gave him a quirky look. "So where would I fit in to all this?" Herzog asked

"What I want you to do, provided you agree to take the job, is investigate this case from the political side of the Hill. Trupp doesn't have the right access. You know your way around that minefield. You would report to me, the same as he does, and never have to deal with anyone else. It will be the ultimate freelance investigator job."

Herzog turned his head and countered, "Why not use one of your career people?"

"This case is too sensitive to go through normal channels. That's why I have a metro guy and hopefully you. We can work faster this way and avoid the political pitfalls that a high profile case like this can generate."

"Translation is, you can control the leaks and not have the investigation get bogged down in beltway bullshit," Herzog responded.

"That's why I always liked working with you Rich. You have an uncanny ability to filter out the crap and get to the point."

Brune parked the car on the street in front of the building. He stuck his Department of Justice sticker on the dashboard, got out, and accompanied his friend through the security door. After they were screened by a metal detector, Brune showed his badge to the security agent and both men signed the register.

They crossed the marble entry foyer and entered the first elevator to their right. Brune pressed the button and the door closed as soon as they were inside. They were the only passengers who rode up to the seventh floor.

"What's the game plan when we get to his office?" Herzog asked.

"I'll show my badge and introduce you as my assistant. That's all these people need to know. We'll meet with the late senator's administrative assistant. I'll start asking the questions and feel free to you jump in any time you want."

Herzog glanced over at Brune. "I haven't told you that I was going to take the job."

"My guess is that after you talk to these people for a while you'll realize that gathering information is a hell of a lot more rewarding than analyzing it. You were the best I ever worked with. I doubt that you've lost your touch."

The two men exited the elevator and walked over to the entrance of Senator Harrington's office. A Capitol guard examined the agent's identification badge and looked down to the appointment schedule. Both men signed in and were allowed to pass.

They stopped at the waist high reception desk. Phones were ringing off the hook and people were scurrying in and out of the various offices that made up the suite. After a couple of minutes they were met by a lady in her sixties, dressed in a navy blue suit. "I'm Mrs. Harriman. May I help you?"

"Yes, I'm Agent Brune from the Justice Department and this is my assistant, Rich Herzog. We have an appointment with the senator's administrative assistant, Miss Boudreaux."

"She's expecting you. Please follow me, and I apologize for the noise level. Things aren't normally like this around here."

"No explanation needed," Brune said as the two men followed her to the back of the office and into a spacious, expensively appointed room. An eight foot wide mahogany wood fireplace with a row of bookshelves formed the east end of the room. A floor to ceiling bookcase formed the rear wall of the office. A six foot cherry red sofa, upholstered in dark plush sat on the left side of the room directly across from a bank of windows. Four matching cherry red wingback leather chairs sat directly in front of an eight foot mahogany desk in the middle of the room.

A tall, redheaded woman in her forties, dressed in a peach-colored designer suit, approached them from behind the desk. "My name is Adrienne Boudreaux," she smiled. "I'm Senator Harrington's administrative assistant. How may I help you gentlemen?"

Brune and Herzog shook her hand and introduced themselves. For a moment Herzog was literally unable to speak. The woman was gorgeous, but there was more to her, some indefinable rightness. The shape of her face, the soft blue eyes, her perfectly proportioned figure—all of these drew the eye. But some extra something commanded all his attention.

He saw Brune turn to look at him. He shook himself out of the spell and smiled back at Adrienne. He felt like a kid trying to get up the nerve to ask a girl out on a date.

"Please sit down," she gestured.

"Thank you," Brune replied. "Ms. Boudreaux, my department is heading up the investigation. I'm going to need a list of everyone who worked for the senator, even the interns."

"I thought you would probably need that so I pulled all the personnel files, past and present."

"I appreciate that. I'm also going to need all of the senator's financial records and campaign contributions, including all the 527 committee money that he received. I also want to have a look at his legislative work, both as committee chairman and as a member of the Banking Committee."

"How far back do you want to go?" she asked.

"The past six years."

"That's going to take awhile, but I can get that for you," she assured him.

"If you would, assemble the information going backward in time, breaking it down in two-year increments. As soon as you get the most recent two-year sessions finished notify me and one of us will pick it up. I want you to treat this as classified information. Keep it in a secure location under lock and key throughout the process."

"Why all the added precautions?" Adrienne pressed.

"Because the media will come snooping around. They'll try to get information from your staff that would compromise our investigation. That's why I want you to limit the number of people who work on the project to a trusted few. I'd like to get the first installment in a couple of days if that's possible."

"I can do that for you. I'll make sure that you have it no later than Friday morning. I've been with the senator for eighteen years and I'll do whatever is necessary to help you out."

"Thank you Ms. Boudreaux. I appreciate that. I have a couple of other items on the agenda that I am going to need as well. I want to see all his phone logs, emails and daily activity calendars for the same time frame."

The administrative assistant told the senior investigator, "I have all that on file, most of it on computer disc. I can have that ready by Friday also. Is there any other information that you need?"

"One last item, I'd like to see his travel itinerary included in the material you are going to have ready by Friday."

"That will not be a problem," she promised.

"Thank you for seeing us this morning, and count on one of us stopping by Friday morning unless we hear from you sooner," Brune told her as they stood up.

"I'll plan on seeing one of you in a couple of days," she nodded as she got up and escorted them to the door. Brune left first. Adrienne made it a point to make sure Herzog saw the engaging look on her face as he left. Herzog returned the gesture on his way out.

After he hooked back up with his former boss out in the hallway, Herzog asked him, "What's the connection between his work and the financial records?"

"I want to see if his legislative agenda follows some kind of money trail. See who he was taking care of. This wasn't a botched robbery and murder of some rich guy in a park by some crack head punk who pumped six bullets into him. This was a murder, plain and simple. I don't know who did it or why right now, but my instincts tell me it is somebody with a history."

"That's why you want to be able to track his movements and contacts every day for the past six years?" Herzog probed.

"So are you on the team or not?" Brune asked as they stepped onto the elevator.

"I want three thousand a week plus expenses. I'm not going to make a career change and take a pay cut at the same time."

"You got a deal," Brune beamed as he shook his hand.

Herzog had a sheepish grin on his face on the way down to the car and it wasn't over the job. He looked at another woman for the first time since his wife's death and didn't feel guilty about it.

Chapter Six

GULFCOAST BANK, SARASOTA
WEDNESDAY 9:30 AM

"Did you catch the news last night Ronnie?" Harper said when he breezed into Gibson's office. "We're in deep shit!"

Harper sat down in one of the black leather chairs in front of Gibson's oak desk.

"I know Martin. David told me about it this morning along with some other bad news," the heavy set, balding partner said as he unclipped his striped tie.

"What's that?" Harper snapped.

"The feds are coming in this week for an audit. A friend of his called and tipped him off. David tried to reach you last night but couldn't get a hold of you."

"Son-of-a-bitch! That means you and David have a lot of work to do. Does he know what day?" Harper said as he took a sip of his tea.

"His friend didn't say."

"Do we have enough cash on hand to cover our deposit base?"

"I think we're covered," Gibson said. "Thomas is bringing in another shipment tonight. I think we'll have enough time to create the necessary paperwork to cover all the money in house. If we can't cover all of it we can move it around from branch to branch until the audit is over. Thomas keeps bugging me about bringing more money in every week. Hell, we're having a hard time getting it all washed as it is," Gibson griped.

"That explains his conversation with me last night," Harper said.

"Why, what did he say?"

"He wants me to take more of it over to Switzerland now that I've opened two more accounts. I did that to spread the risk for all of us, not just for him. I told him that if he wants to do more business with his friends in Panama, we can accommodate them. We'll send it through the new accounts I'm going to set up in the Caymans. That seemed to appease him."

"Well," Gibson sighed, "since he's coming over later, I better start counting the cash on hand this morning and plan on being here late tonight"

Harper took a peek at his watch. "Look, I have meetings downtown all afternoon but I'll come back after we shut down to help out if we need it," Harper offered. "Is David here or did he go out to the new branch?"

"He's still here."

"Sometime in the next couple of days we need to sit down and hatch a new game plan."

Harper left Gibson's office and headed down the hall to his son-in-law. Harper knew that the murder of Senator Harrington was a devastating loss. Their safety net in Washington was gone. His son-in-law had no clue and he couldn't tell him how the Senator had kept the prying eyes of government away.

When he got there, David Dreyer was standing by his desk. Dressed in a dark blue Armani suit, starched white shirt with French cuffs and light blue silk tie, he was the stereotypical corporate banker. A little over six feet tall with a full head of wavy, closely cropped blonde hair, he towered over everyone at the bank, including his boss.

Files were stacked in neat rows in metal bins atop his dark cherry desk. Light blue paint adorned the walls and a couple of ferns decorated the corners. Dreyer's office was an extension of himself: neat and clean, everything in order. Unlike Gibson's office where papers and files were scattered about and the smell of cigar smoke permeated everything.

As Executive Vice President of the bank he headed the retail and commercial small business lending divisions. He was a graduate of the Wharton School of Finance, and had a degree in accounting from the University of Florida. He had married Harper's daughter, Sarah, after graduation and came to work for her father shortly after that.

Dreyer was instrumental in the growth of Harper's S&L operation in Florida as well as his real estate holdings. He had a house in University Park near the golf course, just a couple of streets over from his father-in-law's. Their boats docked in adjacent slips at Siesta Key Marina, though his forty-foot cabin cruiser paled alongside Harper's sixty-footer. Dreyer's was big enough to accommodate his wife and daughters, Jenny and Chloe, for their weekly excursions out on the Gulf of Mexico.

He was living his dream: A wife and family he loved, a job that he was great at and enjoyed and a lifestyle in a city that had everything anyone could possibly want. But lately he was beginning to have reservations about their relationships with lobbyists and politicians in Florida and Washington.

The growing contributions to 527 committees in D.C.—particularly those to John Harrington—troubled him most. Even though these matters were in Gibson's sphere, Dreyer had to deal with them as the bank's in-house accountant. And they implied a question that he couldn't get past: given that the bank was a healthy and growing operation why the need to buy influence? If they just followed the letter of the law and moved on, everything would be fine.

From his point of view all the money going for campaign contributions would be utilized more productively if it were redirected to market research, merger and acquisition data, or product development. All of these were departments within the bank that he was responsible for, that he knew would directly benefit the bank's bottom line. Their market was changing dramatically due to consolidation, the influx of baby boomers into the state and the escalating real estate market. The latter was the greatest worry for Dreyer.

Before long, median-income families would start to be priced out of the market. Creative programs would have to be brought on line to get them back into the stream. That wasn't a priority with his father-in-law, even though he had pushed the idea for some time. It was dismissed, along with most of his other concerns.

Working smarter than everybody else was his mantra for success. But it was becoming harder to do. Instead of investing in their most productive assets, retail and commercial development, Harper had changed its focus to containing operational costs and buying influence.

The unintended consequence was that any short-term gain they might achieve would eventually be offset by losses in service and market share down the road. Dreyer viewed it as the classic case of trying to make money by saving money, versus spending money to grow their business.

Dreyer's faith in Harper was deteriorating as a result of the direction the bank was moving. His father-in-law would always listen patiently when they talked, but David felt the older man was placating him. There was never any real intention to move forward on any of his proposals.

His only option was to keep on working as he had always done, despite the sense that things were closing in around him. Dreyer only spoke to Harper about it in the office when the frustration boiled over, or when he saw something in the market that he felt might move Harper to act. Except for the occasional inquiry about the new branch under construction on Highway 41 Harper never brought it up. That's why he was surprised when Harper knocked on his door early in the morning.

"David, do you have a minute?"

"I was headed over to the new branch as soon as I got my desk cleared off, but I'm in good shape. What's up?"

Harper closed the door behind him and both men sat down.

"You know John Harrington was killed last night and for us it's a huge loss. Without going into a lot of detail, he was in the process of drawing up legislation that would have been a big boost to us. Now it's a moot point. He's dead and so is our main source of protection in Washington. His help with bankruptcy reform and credit-card law were just a couple of things he did for us in the past that made our lives easier."

Dreyer's eyebrows rose. "I didn't know you had worked that closely with him. I knew he was instrumental in getting you the ambassadorship to Switzerland. That he was Ways and Means chairman. But I didn't know you were that close."

"Ronnie and I both go back a ways with him. Ronnie introduced me to him at a charity golf event up at Sawgrass. He went to undergraduate school with him at Virginia. They played on the football team together and stayed in touch over the years.

"That meeting at the golf outing was the beginning of an extremely valuable relationship. One which paid us huge dividends over the years. We talked regularly and I had met with him as recently as last week. Now all that's history," Harper finished. He turned his head and gazed out the window at the inter-coastal waterway a few feet away.

"I've never seen you this distressed. Is there something else bothering you?"

"What do you mean?" Harper asked, clearly caught off guard by the question.

"Did he say or do anything that made you think he had a problem?" Dreyer prodded, wanting to see how his boss responded.

"The senator was his usual self, smiling, telling jokes, having a good old time. We had dinner followed by a couple of drinks at the bar. When I left about 11:30, he walked over and sat down in a booth and began talking with some beautiful red-haired woman. I spent the night at the Four Season Hotel and flew on to Cincinnati the next day. The whole thing just doesn't make any sense." The banker slapped his hand on the desk. "That's what's bothering me so much."

"He helped us out more than I can tell you. Washington is just loaded with bastards who want to pass laws that make our life miserable. Bubba was our guy, the cop on the beat who kept those pricks at bay. My concern going forward is that we're going to have a wave of new banking regulations head our way. Hell, they're already proposing looking into private equity deals and loan syndications deals.

More reporting, more oversight, you name it. We're going to see it," Harper shook his head.

"That brings me to the subject of our deposits and record keeping," Dreyer said. "Caribbean Ventures seems to have an incredible amount of cash in their daily deposit log. I was doing a credit check on Vasquez for a condominium complex he wants to build. For the amount he wants to borrow I have to document his credit score. What's the deal with him?"

"Thomas Vasquez handles a lot of cash through his retail outlets. He does a lot of business with independent contractors. That's the reason for the large cash deposits. Trust me; he has plenty of assets to collateralize the loan if necessary. Ronnie has a handle on it. He's completely legitimate. Don't be concerned about it David," Harper admonished the younger man.

Harper stood up. "I have to get out of here or I'll miss my next meeting downtown. If I don't see you tomorrow, I'll see you at the house for dinner Sunday night?"

"We'll be there."

Harper opened the door and stepped out of the office. Dreyer gazed out through his window at a sailboat passing by on the inland waterway. He shook his head and puffed out a shot of air. The explanation given by Harper didn't come close to satisfying his curiosity concerning Thomas Vasquez, and the way he conducted business.

The tone of his father-in-law's voice told him that all the explanations were a thinly disguised effort warning him to back off. Coupled with the legislation issue that Harper had mentioned in passing raised another red flag. What kind of legislation was Senator Harrington backing that they needed so desperately?

The bank had issues that his boss wasn't sharing with him and Dreyer believed the primary

source was their deposit base and Vasquez. He was
going to have to do a little digging when Harper and
Gibson weren't around.

Chapter Seven
_____

CINCINNATI, OHIO - 9:00 PM

Sherry Novaks relaxed on the deck of her
condominium watching the boats drift by on the Ohio
River. The crafts were illuminated by moonlight as
they passed some five hundred feet below. The sweet
fragrance of lilac blooms wafted across her perch on
the fifteenth floor. Her apartment sat atop the Mt.
Adams hillside and afforded her an unparalleled view
of the Cincinnati skyline and the river valley beyond.

Standing six feet tall and slender she had the
body of a twenty year old model. Her chestnut hair
and fair skin accentuated her good looks. In addition
to her striking appearance she was a woman with
grace and intelligence, all of which had caught Martin
Harper's attention.

Novaks met Martin Harper just after she went
to work as a paralegal in a Cincinnati law firm. He
was one of the firm's biggest clients. They
represented and advised Harper at the early stages
of his banking career. He retained the firm even after
he moved his operations to Florida.

Her affair with him developed despite the fact
that he was married. She found the aura of power that

surrounded him to be irresistible. And he was more than generous; Harper had purchased the condo for her to live in eight years earlier.

Before he moved to Florida they spent a lot of time together there. He had taken her on trips to Switzerland and the Caribbean, and even bought her a BMW Z3 roadster for Christmas several years ago. But life changed for her when he moved to Florida. He wasn't around as much and life was boring.

She still cared for him, but he had another life, a life from which she was excluded. His marriage was a Clinton-like charade that had to be maintained for business and social purposes. After a few years she realized that he was never going to leave his wife, despite his promises to the contrary.

Sherry wanted more and knew that she would never have it with him. She grew tired of her solitary life. Her close circle of friends from high school, now married with families, reinforced her desire for change. There was another world out there that she wanted to be a part of.

After making a hard assessment of her situation she changed things on both personal and professional fronts. She enrolled at the University Of Cincinnati Law School to complete her final year toward a degree and she began to see someone else on a regular basis.

She met Corky Millner, the new love of her life, at Toscani restaurant across the river in Newport, Kentucky. When the tall, dark-haired stranger sitting at the bar next to her struck up a conversation, they hit it off immediately. He called her the next day and they began seeing each other regularly.

Sherry told him up front about her relationship with Harper and that wasn't an issue with him. Both wanted the same thing, a relationship with no permanent commitment. Her primary focus in the short term was getting through law school and at some point away from Harper. Having a social life was the second part, and something of a bonus.

Millner was forty-five and a confirmed bachelor. He dressed the part of a player and had the looks: silk shirts, designer suits, and wavy black hair that was always meticulously cut and groomed. His definition of dating was sex without commitment. The fact that Harper had set her up made it perfect for him. Low maintenance or no maintenance was a way of life for him where relationships were concerned.

His source of money wasn't a concern of hers. She never asked, and he didn't volunteer. As far as she knew he was a gambler who spent most of his days at River Downs or Keeneland race tracks during the season playing the horses. He knew a lot about horses and racing and enjoyed telling stories about the greats of racing, which bolstered her assumption about gambling. That, and the hours he kept.

She had no idea that Millner's real life revolved around his business as a drug dealer who did his thing at night in the bars along the Newport and Covington riverfront. That is where he had access to the professional athletes and the party crowd who made up half his clientele. The rest were small time dealers. Outgoing and friendly, he knew a lot of people on the Cincinnati bar circuit, and they knew him. Only his customers knew what he did for a living.

His relationship with Novaks had evolved to a comfort level that both could handle. She cared for him but not enough to get hurt like she had been with Harper. Now she was able to have a social life. She was able to have dinner and drinks at restaurants and bars with Millner, something she and Harper never did because of his high profile. With her new lifestyle she didn't worry about Harper finding out about the two of them. She ran in circles that Harper didn't know existed.

Other than Harper's driver and his pilots, very few people connected with Harper knew about Novaks. She preferred it that way.

Sherry's life was changing and absolutely for the better. For the first time in a long time she was happy. Her friends saw it and teased her about it when they got together. The nature of her affair with Harper meant she had to keep her social life private. Now with Millner in her life she had the freedom to socialize with her friends as a couple, and she loved every minute of it.

As time went on Harper's visits became less frequent, as did his phone calls. Her ambivalence toward him increased. Out of sight became out of mind. When he did breeze into town, she couldn't wait until he left. Fidelity wasn't the issue; boredom was. Sherry played him like she felt he had played her for the past few years. She still needed him, but not for the reasons he thought. Quite simply, Martin Harper was a means to an end.

Chapter Eight

WASHINGTON, D.C. – THURSDAY 9:00 AM

District Investigator Russell Trupp walked around the corner of the faded granite facade of the Justice Center. A minute later he was following a stream of people into the revolving entry doors of the building. He checked out the directory, went to the elevator and pressed the button for the fourth floor. Charlie Brune's office was the first door on the right. He opened the slate gray metal door and went inside.

"Russell, I would like you to meet Richard Herzog. He's going to be your counterpart out of my office," Brune said.

"Nice to meet you," Trupp said as the two men shook hands. The detective, who was a little shorter than Herzog, was also a little heavier. His receding red hairline and baby face looks belied his fifty years.

"Russ, why don't you bring us up to date on what your forensic team has come up with so far?" Brune instructed.

The three men sat down around an oblong wooden table. Trupp opened his briefcase and laid out some photographs and a couple of computer sheets with charts and graphs. Then he pulled out a legal pad and started sketching.

"Let me begin with the physical evidence. We picked up a couple of cigarette butts and a tiny blood print that matches Harrington's type from the opposite end of the parking lot. Harrington's car was parked here," he tapped on a schematic drawing of the parking lot.

"The Medical Examiner puts the time of death between 9:00 and 10:00. Our office got a call from his Onstar system when the windows of the car were broken out and he didn't respond to his cell phone. That call came in at 9:28. We have a jogger who gave us a description of a car speeding away from the area about the same time. He told one of my investigators he heard an alarm coming from the parking lot a few minutes prior to seeing the car flee the area. The downside is that we weren't able to get any latent prints off of the victim's vehicle."

"What about hair or fiber samples?" Brune asked.

"Sorry, Charlie, we struck out there," Trupp continued, "The blood spray pattern indicates the killer shot them from the passenger-side door, and the windows were up."

"So how was the killer able to sneak up on them?" Herzog asked.

"Based on what little evidence we have my guess is that the killer probably parked at the opposite end of the lot. Then he or she snuck all the way up to the car and shot them through the window," Trupp said.

"They were lying together doing the nasty when it happened. Their blood alcohol levels were point-twelve and point-sixteen. Both were legally drunk. That tells me they probably didn't hear anyone," Trupp said, as he moved one of the pictures of the crime scene over to Herzog.

"The best evidence from the car is a partial bloody footprint from the driver's side. The blood dripped off the door when the killer opened it up. When he stepped up on the running board he left that behind. We did find another trace of it next to the butts we recovered at the other end of the parking lot," Trupp stated.

"By the way, who was the other victim?" Herzog asked.

"You guys aren't going to believe this. Her name was Belinda Hoffman, his twenty-eight-year-old legislative assistant. She has a condo over in Silver Springs. I sent some people over there to check it out."

"Jeez, is there anybody in town this guy wasn't banging?" Brune quipped.

"Only his wife, Annabelle, who spends more time in Charleston than she does here," Trupp chimed in.

"So why not wait twenty minutes and go to her condo?" Herzog asked.

"That's what I keep going back to. My gut instinct says this wasn't Bubba's first trip to the Rock Creek Park 'Motel'. He had to have a certain comfort level with the place or he never would have been there," Trupp offered.

"How often do the Park Police check the area?" Brune asked.

"Not very often," Trupp said.

"Then that lends credence to what you are saying about his comfort level."

"I think the nature of the crime, and the fact that the car wasn't taken tell me it was a premeditated act," Trupp said. "His wallet and her purse were missing, but robbery isn't even a consideration at this point."

Trupp pressed on with his theory. "If you're the perp, and you've already blown two people away, why take the money and not the car? In for a dime in for a dollar. That's how I know it wasn't a robbery gone bad."

"Hmmm," Brune said. "Our next step is going back to his office and talk to his admin. I'll call and let her know we're on our way over. Russ, get back to me if your guys turn up anything at her condo. One more thing, has her family has been notified?"

"Yeah, they live in Richmond," Trupp assured his boss.

"Good, then I can get the media off our ass for a while. My office will have a press release later today detailing what we have up to date. Our cover story is going to be that it was a robbery gone sour. I want to keep the sexual details out of the news. Can we guarantee that, Russ?"

"I've got that covered. I briefed the two officers who were first on the scene and called it in. Nobody else got close enough to see the bodies besides them and my forensic team. Trust me; my forensic team hates news hounds."

"Great, then we can operate as planned. Russ, we'll talk later today. I'm going to be out and about so here's my cell number," Brune said as he handed him a card and a new cell phone.

"By the way, your land line and computer should be up and running by noon."

"My chief called and said they were working on the installation at seven this morning. Thanks for the cell, Charlie," Trupp said.

Brune and the district investigator got up and went over to the door. They spoke briefly and Trupp left. Herzog looked over the evidence file that Trupp had left on the desk. He was particularly interested in the photo array. He stood up and spread them out across the table.

"What are you looking for in that maze?" Brune asked.

"I don't really know. Maybe it's the other car's location that bothers me. Think about it. Maybe it was there when he arrived. If that's the case, then the killer had to walk across the grass embankment and trees that parallel the parking area to get close. Then jump over the split rail fence to the parking lot, and maybe another ten feet to get to the door," Herzog said, astonished at his own conclusion.

The senior agent looked down at the drawings and photographs. "That's why there was no apparent struggle and no other witnesses. We have to assume they were probably the only two cars in the parking lot. This was a well planned murder. Somebody had to do a fair amount of research to pull this off," Herzog told his boss.

"I agree, Rich. Why don't you go over to the Rayburn Building and talk to Ms. Boudreaux?" Brune suggested. "Find out who else he's been sleeping with. It's hard to believe that a guy who was as overweight and overbearing as he was slept around a lot. But that's the reputation he had."

"Do you think she will know?" Herzog asked.

"She'll know. Between herself and Senator Murphy they know everything there is to know about Bubba Harrington. Murphy is head of the Senate Banking Committee and number two on Ways and Means. Harrington was head of Ways and Means and number two on Banking. These boys did more business between them than any other two guys on Capitol Hill. We'll see what Murphy has to say," Brune vouched.

"You want me to talk to Murphy after I finish up at Harrington's office?"

"Give me a call. If I can get away, I'd like to be there with you when you meet with him. In the meantime I'll give him a heads up and let him know someone from my office is coming over to talk to him this afternoon."

"That works. I'm out of here."

Chapter Nine

SENATOR HARRINGTON'S OFFICE - 11:00 AM

"Thanks for seeing me on such short notice," Herzog said as he shook hands with Adrienne Boudreaux. It was dé-jà vu. Once again he was mesmerized by how pretty she was, with her red hair, alabaster skin and high cheek bones. Although she was in her forties she could easily pass for someone hitting thirty. She was a stunning woman with a captivating manner that Herzog could not ignore.

She smiled back, "Anything to help with your investigation Mr. Herzog."

Adrienne gestured toward a wing-backed chair and sauntered behind her desk. "Please be seated. Would you like some coffee or tea?"

"Thank you, no. Ms. Boudreaux."

"Please, call me Adrienne."

Herzog relaxed a millimeter or two while he tried to get it together. He reminded himself of the real reason he was there. Now all he had to do was not piss her off, especially if he ever wanted to see her again.

She continued to smile at him, hoping the agent would relax a little bit.

"All right Adrienne, I need to ask you some very personal questions about the senator."

She interrupted before he could fire off another volley. "I was able to download his travel itinerary from the disc as well as compiling his last two years of meetings, contacts and lunch dates. I stayed late last night with a couple of staffers to finish it up. I knew that you needed it ASAP."

"Thanks. I appreciate your going the extra mile," he told her.

Herzog took in a deep breath, starred at Adrienne, then blurted out, "What I need to know from you is who he was seeing, whether he had slept with anyone in the office and who he had dated in the past."

In a nanosecond the mood changed from something light to something very glum. He looked away. The slender, red-headed woman got up from her seat, turned her back to Herzog without speaking and walked over to a butler's table. She poured herself a cup of coffee and came back to her desk.

The agent summoned enough courage to look her way again. He watched her place the coffee on the glass desk cover, tug at her beige suit coat, and sit down. She took a sip of coffee and glared across the desk before answering him.

"I appreciate people who are direct Richard, but there's a very fine line between being direct and being obnoxious. If you want to know if I slept with my boss the answer is yes. Was it anything more than that? The answer is no, not for him."

He was stunned by her response and tried to defuse the tension in the air.

"I appreciate your honesty. I'm sure that wasn't easy," he said, trying to sooth her hurt feelings.

"Well Richard, may I call you Richard?"

"Please, feel free."

"Why are you asking me about the senator's sex life? Does that mean that you are considering anyone who had a relationship with him a suspect? If that's the case you may have an endless job," she bantered.

Herzog knew what he was about to say was going to blindside her, and he tried to parse his words, but didn't do very well.

"The reason for the question has more to do with the other victim in the car, Belinda Hoffman. That makes this office ground zero. Who else was involved with him?"

"Oh no, Belinda was the woman? That's terrible," she said as she set her cup down and gasped for air.

Herzog felt like an ogre. The interview couldn't be going worse if it had to, and now he had managed to upset her again.

"Adrienne, can you tell me about the other women he dated, starting with this office?"

"Of the current employees it was just the two of us and I didn't even know about Belinda. She must be his latest. The senator and I had a conversation awhile back about not seeing people you work with. That's why I ended our little arrangement."

Herzog adjusted his tie in an effort to let things cool down for a moment while Adrienne took a drink of her coffee.

"What about other women outside the office?" he went on.

"Let me see. There were at least four or five flight attendants. You know, he's a big-time senator. If they're going to have a fling it's going to be with somebody other than the slugs they meet on flights."

Herzog was trying to take copious notes as she droned on. "I also know of a secretary from Senator Murphy's office. Then he had a fling with a real estate broker for quite a while. I'm also guessing he was sleeping with his wife's best friend, Tricia. She was all over him at a party at their house last year that I attended. And that doesn't include the ones he picks up at various watering holes around town. He doesn't go out to drink. He goes out to pick up women."

Herzog resisted the impulse to say something trite.

"Can you get me these people's names and the bars he frequented? At least that gives me somewhere to start."

"Sure, I'll put it with the rest of the information."

"I know this was difficult. You've been a big help," Herzog told her.

"You know, you work with somebody all these years and then they're gone. As hard as it is to accept that, it's even harder to swallow the notion that someone he had contact with could be responsible," she lamented.

"Adrienne, I know we spoke about it yesterday, but I can't emphasize too much the need for confidentiality. Nobody, and I mean absolutely no one, can know the nature of the information that we are seeking from you, or anything I tell you."

"Everything is confidential between us. You have my word. Those vultures from the press corps have been sniffing around like a bunch of dogs in heat. I detest those people," Adrienne railed.

"Good, I'm glad we are on the same page. You have my phone number, and here is my e-mail address. As soon as you get the first two years of his financial and legislative records, please call me or e-mail me."

"I will," Adrienne promised.

Herzog got up, walked around the desk and shook her hand gently. She gazed into his eyes and neither of them moved for a couple of seconds.

Neither said a word as she took her time leading him through the outer office and into the hallway. She smiled and told him goodbye.

When Herzog met her he didn't know if he was getting mixed signals from her, but that wasn't an issue now. And he wasn't feeling conflicted about the prospects of seeing her again.

His cell phone rang and he hit the dial. Charlie Brune was on the other end of the phone.

"Are you still in her office?"

"No, I'm finished and on the way down," Herzog said.

"Stay put, Murphy's office is one floor down. I'll meet you there in about five minutes."

Chapter Ten

RAYBURN OFFICE BUILDING
WASHINGTON DC 12:00 PM

When Brune got off the elevator Herzog was waiting for him outside Senator Murphy's office. The two agents entered the office, identified themselves and signed in. They were met by a blonde college-aged intern at the reception desk. She looked at her appointment log and called back to the Senator's office. The receptionist told him the two agents were waiting to see him. Within seconds she received a call back and escorted them to his office.

"I'm Special Agent Brune, and this is my assistant, Mr. Herzog," Brune said as both men took turns shaking the senator's hand.

"Please be seated," Murphy said.

The two men sat down in beige-colored cloth chairs in front of Murphy's desk. He wore a grey suit, white shirt and dark green tie. His salt and pepper hair, and thin frame disguised his age.

His office was utilitarian. A desk and computer were surrounded by wooden bookshelves that spanned the west wall. A bank of windows was on the opposite side. At the far end of the room, a plasma television sat on the left side of the wall with an oak table and four chairs in front of it. On the right side was a glass cabinet filled with wine, liquor and glasses. The soft, dark green carpeting that covered the floor was the only item in the room that was dated.

The senator peered across the desk and said, "It's a tragedy about John Harrington. Is anybody safe in this town anymore?"

Brune shot back, "Senator Murphy, you worked with him longer and more closely than anyone else on the hill. Did Senator Harrington ever express concern over his safety?"

"No, he didn't." Murphy gave him a quizzical look and added, "But I thought this was a robbery or attempted car-jacking. That's what the press reported."

"That's not what happened. But before we go any further I have to ask you to promise something. What we say here stays here. I'll keep you up to date as a courtesy because of your relationship with the senator. But I want to keep the media out of it. Do we have an agreement?"

"Yes we do, gentlemen. Now tell me what really happened," Murphy demanded.

"He was shot to death along with his legislative assistant in Rock Creek Park. We know he attended a party at the Israeli Embassy and left around 8:30. They were both found shot in his car, we think by a jogger, an hour later."

"Any witnesses, anybody hear gunshots?"

"No. We have some leads we're working on, but that's it. The victims' wallet and purse were missing, but we don't think robbery was the motive. The position of the bodies at the crime scene tells us otherwise."

The senator leaned forward in his chair and asked, "What the hell are you saying?"

"They were having sex. He was shot in the back of the head and there were no signs of a struggle," Brune told him.

Murphy slumped back in his chair and shook his head before blurting out, "Good God!"

"That's why we need your help. We're trying to establish a motive and work back from that point. Unfortunately, with the limited amount of physical information at hand we have to cover a lot of ground. We want to look at everything you gentlemen worked on, both in his committee and yours. We need pending legislative reports, financial reports, and campaign contributions, including the 527 committees."

Murphy stared back across the desk and his jaw dropped.

"I know we are casting a wide net Senator, and some of it is confidential information, but we have to have it all. And we have to be able to investigate this out of the media limelight. That is your guarantee that the information we receive from you will never be page one news."

The senator leaned forward and exhaled. "Well, since we are speaking in confidence there are some things you need to know about Bubba Harrington. I mean besides the obvious fact that he couldn't keep his fly zipped up."

Brune and Herzog were taken aback by the comment. The lead agent asked, "Such as?"

"John Harrington ran Ways and Means like a feudal lord," he told the two investigators. "He curried favor with people using money or legislative blackmail. He ruled with an iron fist. If somebody didn't fall in line he shut them down. He would do his level best to make sure they got shitty committee assignments and no campaign money. John was a real bastard," Murphy finished.

Brune and Herzog sank back in their chairs, surprised again by the content and tone coming from the Kentucky Senator.

"What about his word?" Brune asked.

"If John Harrington told you something, you could take it to the bank. That's also where the fear and respect came from. When he asked for something and didn't get it, he got pissed and the offending party could count on retribution," the senator affirmed.

"Did the same hold true for lobbyists and campaign contributors?" Brune wanted to know.

"Even more so for them. His position as committee chairman allowed him to be the biggest fund raiser on the Hill. When he called, people ponied up."

Brune leaned forward in his chair and probed a little more. "Are you aware of any instance where he asked for money, and he didn't deliver on his promise?"

"I'm sure there were some instances where that happened, but he never told me about a specific case. Bubba used to talk about reeling in a fish once in a while. About how he would hit up some constituent for a big contribution, then push back the legislation to the next term so he could reel them in again.

The lead agent asked, "Are you aware of any specific case where that happened in the last couple of sessions?"

"I could probably dig up some information on legislative proposals that were tabled, and resurrected the following year. But he was the one who dished out the cash. You would have to be able to look at a contribution list and compare it to the legislative side."

"Did he sponsor much legislation out of his committee," the senior investigator asked.

"No, the majority of it was done by proxy."

"So his name was never on a dicey piece of legislation coming out of committee?" Brune offered.

"No, his name was rarely on any piece of legislation that came out. That was the carrot-and-stick approach he used. Do it, or else."

"The same hold true for proposals that came over to banking?" Herzog piped in.

"Pretty much."

Brune gathered his thoughts then told Murphy, "Senator, we'd like to get information going back at least six years, as quickly as possible. With particular emphasis on the last two sessions."

"We're in recess so my staff isn't exactly overburdened at this time of year. I'll give you a call as soon as I have the first part of it ready."

"Thank you, Senator. We appreciate your candor," Brune told him as he and Herzog got up from their chairs. The men shook hands with Murphy and he escorted them to the outer office.

As the door closed behind them and they exited into the hallway, the senior agent looked at Herzog and stated, "We caught a break with Murphy. He didn't like Harrington. He only tolerated him because he had to."

"I agree there was no love lost between these two, at least not from Murphy's side."

People on Capitol Hill derisively referred to the two of them as a couple of good old country boys, especially Harrington. That's where the name Bubba came from. But after meeting with Murphy, Brune knew there was more to it. "My gut tells me this guy is no wheeler dealer. He's a straight shooter who can lead us in the right direction," he said confidently.

Chapter Eleven

SARASOTA, FLORIDA - 8:00 PM

David Dreyer finished the last of his documents and was entering the information on his computer. Ronnie Gibson knocked on his open door, popped his head inside and asked, "How much longer are you going to be?"

"I was just wrapping it up. What about you?"

"I probably have another hour to go on the computer and then I have to count the cash in the vault. If you were going to be here a while, I was going to suggest we take a break and have a drink."

"Thanks Ronnie, but I have to get home. It's my daughter Chloe's birthday today."

"Have a good night David," Gibson said as he strolled back down the hall to his office.

When the disc popped out of his computer, Dreyer placed it in a plastic case and put it inside his briefcase. He turned off his computer, grabbed his jacket and flipped the light switch as he hustled out the door.

Dreyer pressed the remote button for his Lexus and looked around the parking lot. The only car remaining was Gibson's cranberry-colored Porsche

911. He pulled out of the bank onto Highway 41 and headed north. As he pulled up to the light at Clark Road, he realized that he had left Chloe's present back at the office. He made a quick U-turn on the south berm and sped back to the bank.

Five minutes later he was back on Stickney Point Road near the entry lane for the bank. He slowed down and made the turn past the ground-level bank sign at the north end of the parking lot. As he approached, something behind the bank caught his eye. He stopped suddenly. "What the hell?" he muttered.

He turned his lights off and backed the car up behind the vegetation barrier to avoid being seen, then turned off the ignition. Dreyer got out of the car. He squatted down and peeked around the last tall bush. Two men were unloading dark colored duffel bags from a white fleet van while a third watched. They were about a hundred and fifty feet away, but Dreyer thought he recognized the third man when he turned and looked into the darkness. He knew Gibson was still at the bank, but it wasn't him. Dreyer ducked back quickly behind the cover of the hedges.

A couple of seconds later he peered out again. When he did, two of the men entered the bank and slipped behind the teller counter. The as yet unidentified man was gesturing to Ronnie Gibson, who had stepped out of the darkness. The men with the bags followed Gibson back to the vault area while the stranger unlocked the back of the van, and lit a cigarette.

Dreyer's worst fears were confirmed. It was Thomas Vasquez.

Dreyer ducked out of sight, trying to decide what to do. When he heard voices again, he looked out and saw the men lug two more duffel bags into the bank. They repeated the process three more times, after which Vasquez closed the van door and carried the last full bag himself.

The banker got back inside his car and started the engine. Lights off, he backed along the entry way and prayed that no one else would turn down the one-way lane. No one did.

Back at the street entrance he waited for the traffic to lighten up and backed out into the street. When he got a break he shot into the center lane and roared past the banking center, hoping the cars on the inside lane shielded his getaway from anyone at the bank.

He loosened his tie and lowered the window. His heart was pounding and beads of perspiration began rolling down his forehead. He dialed his cell phone.

"Sarah, I am on my way. I'll explain why I'm late when I get home."

"David, where are you? You should have been home a half an hour ago. Chloe is waiting to open her presents. It's bad enough you missed dinner."

"I'm sorry. I got hung up at work, and had to go back because I forgot her present."

"David, I called your office and you didn't pick up. And your cell phone was turned off too. I don't want to hear any more. Just get home."

"Hello, hello. Great!" He dropped the phone on the passenger seat. "Now what the hell am I going to do?"

He had twenty minutes to figure out what he could say to his wife, and what he had to say to his daughter. He had no present and no excuse—unless he wanted to tell his wife what happened.

A Shop-Mart sign loomed ahead. Dreyer wheeled into the parking lot. He hustled into the store and ran back to the stereo department. He told the clerk he wanted Kenny Chesney's CD, *When the Sun Goes Down*. The clerk unlocked the case and handed him the CD. He ran to the front of the store to the checkout line where he slid to a stop at the end of a line of shoppers.

"Damn," he said to himself. "Why are there always ten people in line and only three registers open at this place?" He alternated between looking at his watch and counting the number of items each shopper was buying until it was his turn to check out.

When the ordeal was finally over he was out of the parking lot and back on University Parkway like a shot. His mind kept replaying the scene at the bank with Vasquez and all the duffel bags.

The crux of the issue was how to handle it going forward. He loved his wife dearly, but any information he gave to her was only a conversation away from his father-in-law. He decided to take the path of least resistance for the present time, not tell her at all and take the heat.

That solved the first part of the puzzle. The second was a bit harder. Since Gibson ran the operational end of the bank, Harper had to know what was going down. He had to know there were duffel bags full of cash coming into the bank, unless Gibson was running a side game. That seemed like a bit of a stretch given Gibson's lack of ambition, but the only way to confirm it would be to get his father-in-law alone and press his buttons and see how he reacted.

The information that he needed to see regarding deposits and withdrawals was guarded like a state secret by Gibson. But the red flag had been raised by Dreyer earlier when he asked Harper about Caribbean Ventures, Vasquez' holding company and their unusually large deposits base. His dismissive response didn't seem out of the ordinary at the time, but after tonight it made perfect sense.

Chapter Twelve

CHEVY CHASE, MARYLAND – 8:15 PM

With the background music and the voices filling his living room, Charlie Brune didn't realize his cell phone was ringing until it had chirped out its pattern four times. He snagged it from his belt to find Russell Trupp on the line.

"Sorry to bother you at home," the homicide investigator apologized, "but I have some information."

"That's not a problem. Hold on, I have to go outside to talk to you. We have a house full of people... I'm OK now, go ahead," Brune told him.

"We found the car that was in the parking lot the night Harrington was killed. Hotel security at the Best Western in Roslyn called in a report about an abandoned vehicle, and we caught a break. We were able to get positive DNA matches from Harrington in the killer's car from a blood smear on the floor mat. And we got a DNA match from cigarette butts we recovered from the crime scene that match those in the car at the hotel," the investigator told his boss.

"Great work, Russ," he applauded.

"I also have people checking the surveillance cameras from the hotel parking lot and from the metro station a couple of blocks away," Trupp added.

"Do you think our killer might be a local?" Brune asked.

"I don't know. We'll search the area and talk to cabbies and bus drivers to see if anyone picked up a fare that night. If we can get a picture off a video camera from either the hotel or the subway platform, that would be huge."

"Don't hesitate to call me. See you in the office tomorrow. Tell your crew, good work," the Justice agent said.

"Catch you tomorrow, Charlie."

Chapter Thirteen

CINCINNATI, OHIO - 8:15 PM

Sherry Novaks had just shut the balcony screen behind her when the phone rang. With a small sigh of exasperation she stood and stepped inside to answer it. She never could remember to take it out with her.

"Hello?"

"Sherry, this is Martin." His voice sounded tense.

"Well, this *is* a nice surprise." It had been long enough since she'd heard from him that she put a little irony in her voice to make him wonder if she were upset with him. "What's going on?"

"I'm not going to be able to see you Saturday. I have to fly to Washington for a funeral. Sorry honey, I was really looking forward to seeing you." The words poured out as if he feared her reaction.

"So was I. So when do you think you will be able to get up here?" Novaks asked.

"I don't know. There's a lot going on at the bank, and I have to fly down to the Caribbean next week for a meeting. Everything is up in the air for the next few weeks. Look, I have to get going. Daddy loves you. I'll call next week. Night."

"Love you too. 'Night." She broke into grin from ear to ear and strolled out of the bedroom onto the patio deck with her glass of Disaronno liqueur. Her black silk nightgown was flowing in the soft summer breeze coming across the river basin. She set her drink on the glass table and kissed Corky as they stood against the railing.

"God, you feel good tonight," he said as he stroked the back of her neck.

"So do you," she giggled. "I have some terrific news to share with you. We're good to go all week. He can't come up this weekend, or next. That's awesome!"

"Damn, that is good news. I'm having a hell of a week. I hit the daily double at River Downs a couple of days ago, and closed a deal in Miami this morning. Now this. We have to go out and celebrate tomorrow," Millner said.

"I agree. Let's have dinner at Boca. You know I like to celebrate with Italian, and you can't get any more Italian than that. I'll call and make reservations tomorrow. Does eight o'clock work?"

"Yeah, that sounds good. I've never been there," Millner told her.

"Well, I have. The food is great—*real* Italian, like being in Tuscany, but enough about that. Let's go inside and really celebrate," Novaks said as she took his hand and headed for her bedroom.

Chapter Fourteen

GULFCOAST BANK, FLORIDA - 8:30 PM

"Sorry I didn't get back sooner, but the damned meetings took forever," Harper said as he locked the bank door behind him. "Thomas may be fronting our new high rise but I have to do all the grunt work. The investment consortium we've put together for the project is different than anything we've done in the past. But he thinks everything should run on cruise control."

The bankers went into Gibson's office and sat down. "Is anybody getting antsy?" Gibson asked.

"Not yet, but we're going to have an issue with the cash crunch because the units aren't selling fast enough. The bank still has to continue making interest payments to the investors regardless of how many units are sold. We can't default on the interest payments to them. Eventually all the units will sell, but that won't generate enough cash to keep up in the short term. That's why we're going to set up some more accounts in the Caribbean."

"So what are you saying? That we're going to use Gulfcoast as a piggy bank?" Gibson asked.

"That's exactly what I am saying Ronnie. You told me we've had our ass handed to us in the derivative markets. We sure as hell can't recoup our losses in the equities market in the near term because every time one of those bastards in Washington opens their mouth stocks go in the tank. The only area where we're making good money is in David's sector with our loan portfolio. And there's not enough of a revenue stream to tap that plus cover everything else. So we don't have any choice but to keep moving the money around until we can right the ship."

"So what do we do to cover the short-term obligations like the interest payments you were talking about?" Gibson wanted to know.

"I gave Thomas the green light to launder more money. Park it here until the audit is over; then move it through the Caymans, Antigua and Tortola in addition to Switzerland and Liechtenstein. I plan to set up new accounts up in the Caymans and Tortola next week when I'm down there. Then we send it back through Antigua, Switzerland and Lichtenstein. By using the float we can buy the time necessary to cover the checks we have to write," Harper said.

"In essence we're going to use Thomas' money to cover our debt."

"That's the only answer for now. He trusts us and being able to launder more money will make him a hero with his friends back in Panama and Columbia. I set the whole thing up over dinner the other night. He bought into it hook, line and sinker. And we still get our ten percent cut," the senior banker finished, a sly grin on his face.

"As far as the audit goes, we look good," Gibson said. "Thomas brought in enough cash to cover what our deposit base should be and I purged our investment portfolio, except for the money makers."

"So on paper we're still solvent?"

"Just like the day you bought it," Gibson guaranteed.

"I need a drink. Do you want to share some Maker's Mark?" Harper asked as he opened Gibson's liquor cabinet behind his desk.

"I believe I will."

Harper poured two glasses, and the two men sat back in their leather chairs and sipped their whiskey in silence. As he finished his bourbon, he told Gibson the funeral was on Saturday.

"I had Kevin file the flight plan today. We'll leave after we close up shop tomorrow night. Then we'll come back Saturday night if everything works out. No need to be around all those bastards that want to cut our nuts off."

"I'll drink to that," Gibson said as he pounded down the shot.

Chapter Fifteen

DEA OFFICE, MIAMI, FLORIDA -11:00 PM

The slate gray BMW 745LI pulled up to the metal entry gate and stopped next to the guard shack. The driver's side window slid down as the security guard leaned toward the window. He recognized the man behind the wheel and waved the car through the wrought iron metal gate and into the compound.

After the car cleared the gate it rolled smoothly closed behind him. The vehicle, a recent forfeiture picked up in a drug bust over on the west coast, was just one element of DEA Agent Jorge Guzman's elaborate cover.

With his shiny grey suit, a black, open-collared shirt and gold chains dangling around his neck the undercover cop looked every inch the slick dealer. But when he got out of the car, opened the back door and grabbed the handcuffed prisoner by the scruff of the neck, his demeanor changed. He was transformed into what he was, a tough DEA agent bringing in his first prize since he got the new set of wheels.

"Do you need any help with the prisoner, sir?" a voice from the guard shack asked.

"No thanks, Alberto. I can take care of this weasel by myself."

Guzman helped the prisoner slide out of the seat and stand up. The guard stared back at the man in the grey uniform as Guzman hit the keypad and entered the building. They took the elevator up to the third floor. From their cubicles scattered across the floor of the outer office other agents watched as the two men walked back to the office of Commander Ron McPherson.

"Boss, we nabbed the first link in the chain of guys we're after."

"Sit down, dirt bag," Guzman told the prisoner as he put his arm on his shoulder and pushed him down in the metal chair. "I set him up the other day, then got him today on film taking an envelope full of hundreds from a couple of guys driving a powder blue 1980 Caddy convertible. I got their plates and pictures too."

McPherson studied the prisoner. He saw a short, heavy-set, balding man in a customs uniform. "Where did you pinch him?" McPherson demanded.

"Outside the customs clearing terminal. He was the only agent working the shift. I hopped the fence and followed him to the rear of the building. He went over to a container with a manifest, checked the number, put the seal on it and walked to the front desk. Then he made a phone call."

Guzman handed McPherson a manila envelope with all the information he found at the warehouse. "Everything's there, the container manifest, the phone number of the consolidator, the cash, and the surveillance film."

McPherson opened the door and called out to one of the agents in the cubicles. A couple of seconds later he was standing at the door.

"Run this information down and get back to me right away," McPherson said as he handed the folder to the agent, then turned back to Guzman. "So who's guarding the container?"

"I got a couple of guys from Metro Dade sitting on the place. Nobody's going in to pick anything up until I say. The consolidator isn't coming around until he gives them a call, according to our friend here." Guzman poked a finger on the prisoner's chest. "Right, Agent Osborne?"

"That's what I told you before," the hapless customs agent replied. "I don't know anything else. Somebody gave me a couple of bucks to get the container out of there in a hurry. That's all I'm guilty of."

"You're a lying sack of shit. I'm guessing these guys are foreign nationals. If they are we can hold you indefinitely under the Patriot Act. Because as far as we know, you could be aiding and abetting terrorists."

Grinning, Guzman paced in front of Osborne. "Doesn't matter whether its weapons, drugs, or money, we've got your sorry ass. You don't even get a phone call. We can have you jailed and shipped out of the country by the weekend. Officially you will be listed as just another missing person in Miami," Guzman barked at the prisoner as he walked over to the water cooler and got a drink.

By now Osborne's grey uniform was soaked with perspiration, and the agent began to squirm in his chair. McPherson reached behind his back and unlocked his metal handcuffs. The prisoner rubbed his wrists, then cupped his hands and put them to his lips.

"My agents hate guys like you who are supposed to be protecting this country from terrorism and drug dealers," McPherson said.

"In fact, they normally beat the hell out of them before they bring them in. So look at it this way. You've been given a pass. Be smart and make the most of it by telling us everything about your little operation. Maybe you'll only do three-to-five up in Atlanta. Who knows what the alternative is if you don't cooperate?"

"What do you want to know?" the customs agent asked in a dull voice.

"Everything, dirt bag," Guzman yelled back at him.

"Any chance of getting into the witness protection program?"

"That depends on your continued level of cooperation," McPherson replied.

Guzman closed the office door, grabbed a chair and sat down two feet from the agent's face. McPherson sat on the edge of his desk and pressed the button on the tape recorder. "Tell us what you know, starting with your name."

"My name is Michael Osborne. A couple of Columbians came to me a while back and I started doing favors for them."

"You mean two total strangers just came over to your house one day, you invited them in, and presto, you're in business with them?" Guzman feigned disbelief.

"Not exactly," Osborne hedged.

"Listen, you're not some freaking Sunday school preacher getting paid by the word. So get to the point and tell us what hook these guys used to get your stupid ass on their payroll," Guzman boomed as the veins in his neck popped.

"All right, I get the drift. No need to be hostile."

Osborne loosened the top button on his shirt, licked his lips, and began to speak again.

"I met them at Hialeah. I go there at least once a week, and usually hit one of the patio bars close to

the track afterwards and shut it down. So I'm over at
the bar one night after a pretty good pay day at the
track, and I fired up a joint. These two guys see me
and come over. At first I thought they were narcs, but
then they offered me some of their stuff to try. Man, it
was great shit."

Guzman and his boss traded looks and rolled
their eyes. "That's it?" Guzman shouted, palms up in
the air

"No, there's more. We spent the rest of the
night drinking rum and Cokes and getting stoned. I
woke up the next morning in a hotel room with a
naked 14-year-old Cuban girl and two vice cops at
the foot of the bed. I don't remember how either of us
got there."

"Go on, what happened next?" Guzman
prodded.

"After they took a couple of pictures they
started asking questions and I showed them my
identification. They believed my story and told me
they'd cut me a break. Professional courtesy, they
said. So I got to walk. They took the girl with them
because she was a juvenile. Everything was cool for
a couple of weeks."

"Then what?" the undercover agent asked.

"I stayed away from the track and hung around
the house on my off days. Two weeks to the day after
the incident a courier comes knocking on my door. He
handed me a package that I had to sign for. Thank
God my wife wasn't home, because when I open it up
there's a picture of me and the naked girl together in
the motel room with a note."

Guzman smirked and shook his head. "Don't
stop now, I'm hanging on every word."

"Like I was saying, the package had a note
and the note said I wasn't to talk to anyone. That I
was to be at a phone booth across from the office
where my wife works on Collins Avenue at 3 o'clock

that afternoon. If I didn't show they said they were going to deliver the pictures to my wife and to my boss."

"Slick bastards, these friends of yours," Guzman said as he mockingly smiled at him.

"I did what they said and went to the phone booth. They called me at 3 o'clock on the button. I met them at the racetrack parking lot an hour later. They gave me a choice. Either join them and make a grand every other week, or my life as I knew it was going to be over."

"Then what?" Guzman asked

"I agreed to do what they wanted. It was pretty simple. They would give me the manifest number and the date of the container's arrival. In return I would make sure I was working when it came in. All I had to do then was clear it and call the freight expediter or them, depending on what they wanted to do. They paid me a thousand dollars every other week."

"Always the same two guys?" McPherson asked. "What about their bosses?"

"Man, I've never seen or talked to nobody else. Just the two guys in the powder blue Cadillac convertible."

The two agents moved away from Osborne, out of hearing distance. Just as they were about to confer another agent rapped on the door and was waved in. He handed McPherson a folder, turned, and walked out, closing the door behind him.

"We got a hit on the driver," the head agent said, huddling with Guzman. "His name is Pedro Estacio. He lives over in Coconut Grove. At least we know where to pick him up. Let's see if he shows up tomorrow to claim his goodies. Is this guy supposed to be working tomorrow?"

"I don't know, I'll ask him," Guzman said. He turned to Osborne, "Hey! Are you supposed to be there tomorrow and meet them?"

"Yeah, I always come in the day of the pickup just to make sure there isn't a problem."

"Then you and I are going to work tomorrow, and you get to wear a two way microphone."

"You can't do that. These guys will kill me if they even think I'm wearing a wire."

The undercover agent got in Osborne's face. "Well, you're going to have to be real careful now aren't you, and not do anything stupid? We're going to hear everything so don't try and warn them. In fact, we're going to tell you what to say."

He caught a look in the prisoner's eyes and said, "And yeah—we'll try to keep you alive. Now stand up so I can put your bracelets back on," Guzman ordered.

"I'll take him into the back office and cuff him to the bed. I want to keep a low profile with this guy. Tomorrow morning he can get cleaned up before we take him over to the warehouse. Then it's show time."

"Let me know if you need any help tomorrow morning," McPherson offered.

"Nah, I'm good. I'll take Davis and Rodriquez with me. I'll be back in the office at seven," Guzman told his boss as he led Osborne to the bunk room.

Chapter Sixteen

WASHINGTON, D.C. – SATURDAY 9:00 AM

"Sorry about the early start," Brune told his men. "But with Harrington's funeral and all today I wanted to make sure we touched base before Rich had to leave. Russ, can you update us on your end of the investigation."

"I've been at the office since seven-thirty, Charlie. This doesn't cramp my style. I can't speak for Rich, though."

Herzog laughed and replied, "I get up at six and run. It helps clear my mind for the day."

"Yeah, I get the point. I'm the late sleeper who gets to the office at nine. So what do you have?" Brune asked.

"We got a picture from the subway surveillance camera in Roslyn. Looks like a match on our guy who parked the car at the Best Western. We compared those two pictures with one from a camera at Reagan airport. The subway and airport pictures are a positive ID. The hotel picture is a little fuzzy because of the distance and the time of night, but my lead investigator believes it's him," Trupp said.

"Any lead on where he flew?" the agent in charge asked.

"We looked at the time sequence from American, United and Delta, and matched it with their passenger boarding cameras. They were the only airlines who had flights leaving between eleven and midnight. His picture came up on an American flight manifest to Miami. The gate agent remembered him. There were only three people in first class and he was one. His name is Carlos Batista."

"Good work, Russell," Brune said.

"Peggy Timmons, one of my investigators, called me from the airport when she got the information. So it's hot off the presses. Charlie, I figured your office could run it down through NCIC."

The agent took the manila envelope and asked, "What about the dead girl's condominium?"

"Other than a couple of love letters he wrote to her we pretty much struck out there. He's been seeing her for a while, according to the doorman. Harrington slipped him a couple of hundred-dollar bills now and then to keep his mouth shut. That's about it. We're doing a check of her phone records to see if that turns up anything. Her parents are coming back tomorrow to clear out her condo, so we have to finish up today. This looks like a dead end to me," Trupp said.

"What about Harrington's phone records and anything else from up on the Hill?" Trupp asked his boss.

"Rich is supposed to get those today. We had a heart-to-heart talk with his number one buddy, Senator Murphy. He said he was a real bastard with enemies in Congress and probably outside as well. He was a big-money guy spreading the cash around to the chosen few. We'll have a better picture when we go through his financial records, which we're going to get today. I think we may have to talk to some other folks up on the Hill."

"I'm going over to get the first installment of his financial records this morning from his admin," Herzog said. "In fact, I have to get over there right away. She told me that she has to leave for the funeral by ten."

"All right then, we'll meet back here Monday at nine unless I hear from one of you. Russ, I'll e-mail you the information about Batista as soon as I get it."

"I'm out of here. See you Monday."

"Rich, if you find anything that looks interesting give me a call. In the mean time I'll see what I can dig up on our friend from Miami."

"See you Monday Charlie," Herzog said.

Chapter Seventeen

GULFCOAST BANK - 9:00AM

David Dreyer parked his car behind the building and entered the bank through the back door. His pulse quickened as he tapped the security code into the keypad. The door opened, and he stepped inside quickly and looked out the window to make sure that no one was in the parking lot.

Part of him felt like a criminal, invading the empty bank on a Saturday morning. He had no choice if he wanted to get the information he needed. Since Harper and Gibson were at Harrington's funeral in Washington this was the best shot he had.

He was hoping that he could round up the information, put it on a disc and be out within the hour. If not, then he had a problem. He couldn't open the vault, but Ronnie Houston's computer was another matter.

Dreyer lucked out and picked up Gibson's password the previous week while they were both closing up. Gibson left his office for a couple of minutes and Dreyer stepped inside to ask him a question and saw the password on the computer screen. He silently backed out the door. A couple of seconds later Gibson came around the corner and the two men spoke, the latter unaware of the discovery.

Dreyer rifled Gibson's desk drawer with a letter opener and found the keys to his file cabinet. He was able to get it open, but he struck out. He found no relevant information. Dreyer went back to Gibson's computer, brought up the login screen and punched in the password "Victoria." He smiled as the program opened, he could have guessed that one. It was one of Ronnie's old girlfriends.

He scrolled down to the accounts section and typed in "Caribbean Ventures." A spread sheet came up, listing various deposits and the shell companies Gibson transferred money to and from. Dryer pulled a disc from his jacket and slid it into the computer.

As the computer copied the information, he jotted notes down on a yellow legal pad. Cayman Islands, Switzerland, Panama, Antigua and Lichtenstein were the locations. Development projects, shell companies with foreign addresses, subsidiary companies with Post Office Box numbers for addresses, it was all there. The dollar amounts moved in and out every month were in the millions. More than could be generated by Vasquez' existing legitimate business interests.

"I knew it! That son-of-a-bitch is nothing more than a money launderer," Dreyer shouted as he slammed his fist on the desk.

He downloaded the file, ejected the disc and slid it into his jacket. Then he scrolled down to the profit-and-loss statement of the bank. After reading through it for a few minutes he sneered and said, "This is total bullshit!"

The investment portfolio he reviewed was a fraction of what he thought it should be, and there was no record of the derivative trades that he knew

Gibson had made. The commercial and residential loans for which he was responsible were the only factual parts of the document. He wondered if the bank was even solvent.

Dreyer turned the computer off and sat in the chair staring at the blank screen.

"How in the hell did we ever get to this point? Being a clearing house for money launderers," he whispered to himself.

There was no mistaking what he had seen the other night. All three of those bastards had to be in bed together for this to have gone on for so long. No wonder Martin shut him down when he bought up his concerns about Vasquez.

He reflected back to what his father told him after his graduation from Wharton; "that in this life two things rise to the top, cream and bastards. Don't be one of the latter." That obviously didn't apply to his father-in-law.

Dreyer respected and emulated his father, a hard working, self-employed business man. Honesty and hard work were the keys to success in life. Do that and you will always be happy, the elder Dreyer had told his son

So why wasn't that good enough for Harper? Why did he have to be fabulously rich, and in the process ruin the lives of his family? Dreyer had been used by his father-in-law, and he was seething. But he reserved some of that anger for himself for being naïve. From day one he had sensed that Harper was self absorbed and power hungry, which he was, but he was also manipulative.

The rumors about the girl friend back in Cincinnati that he chose to ignore and all the trips out of the country should have hit him like neon lights. He was surrounded by crooks every day for years. How could he have not connected the dots? Someone with this many character flaws had to have an outside agenda.

Dreyer pounded his fist on the table. "That miserable bastard! How could he do it?" he shouted.

He grabbed a coffee cup from the top of the desk and hurled it against the wall, shattering it to pieces.

He was screwed. All of Dreyer's suspicions were confirmed in spades. The only unresolved issue was how to proceed. He knew he had to keep his wife out of the equation for his family's safety. Dreyer was furious that his father-in-law had put his family at risk to cover his ass. A lifetime of work was down the drain, and probably his reputation as well. Everyone in management at the bank would be painted with the same broad brush once the default and money laundering came to light. A classic case of guilt by association.

In the midst of his anger Dreyer found inspiration; he would take Harper down.

In the short term all he could do was maintain the charade of ignorance. Act like nothing had changed, like he was still a team player. Pound the pavement and continue to make bucks for the bank. Until he was ready to go to the feds with what he knew, he would resist saying anything to his wife. But he was going to get Harper's ass.

The first order of business was to secure the information he had gathered by placing it in a safe-deposit box, off-site. He could do that on Monday over at the Provident Bank branch on Beneva Avenue.

Dreyer picked up the broken shards of the cup and left the room. He punched in the security code and slammed the metal door behind him. The noonday sun blasted him in the face distorting his vision. When his vision cleared he made out a couple of guys in suits standing next to a dark-blue Ford sedan parked behind his car.

The surprised banker stopped in his tracks and asked, "Who are you, and what do you want?"

"Sarasota Police Department," the taller one said. "What are you doing here?"

"My name is David Dreyer. I'm an officer with the bank," Dreyer said, as he reached inside his coat pocket.

They looked at his bank ID tag.

"Have a nice day, Mr. Dreyer," the tall one said.

Dreyer put his identification tag back inside his jacket and walked past them to his car. As he watched them drive away, he found himself wondering why they were there in the first place. Had Martin Harper called them to check up on him? Or was he being paranoid?

As the Sherlock Holmes tales used to say, the game was afoot.

But the game couldn't end too soon.

Chapter Eighteen

WASHINGTON, D.C. - 10:00 AM

The limousine ride from the Embassy Suites Hotel in Arlington to the Washington Cathedral on Wisconsin Avenue took less than a half hour. Unlike Gibson, Harper seemed agitated and spoke very little during the trip. When they got to the Cathedral Ronnie Gibson got out first and headed for the entrance of the church. Harper followed him. They stopped just before they reached the area cordoned off for the hearse.

A small group of people stood at the base of the steps. Gibson stopped short of joining them and waved Harper to the far right of the stone staircase. He lit a cigarette. "What's bothering you, Martin? You didn't say ten words on the way over here."

Harper glared at him. "First of all, I don't really want to be here, and secondly I think there may be a problem with David. When I called my daughter to confirm that we were going to get together tomorrow, she told me that David had gone over to the bank this morning on some business. He never goes in on a Saturday. Never!"

Gibson blew a cloud of smoke out, turned his head to Harper and said, "So what's the problem?"

"I have no idea. I know one thing, he's been acting odd lately. Not his usual self at the bank. Have you noticed?"

"Not really," Gibson replied.

"Sarah confirmed what I observed, namely that he's been acting strange. He was late for my granddaughter's party the other night. She said that he's had very little to say to her lately, and he's been very withdrawn. And earlier this week he was asking me questions about the nature of Thomas' business. Then today when both of us are gone he decides to go to the office."

"Sounds like he's got a burr up his ass. We better find out what he's up to," Gibson said.

"You said all the bank records were in good shape, but can he access any old information, or anything on Thomas?" Harper asked.

"No. I downloaded all the information to discs and have them in a vault at my house. My active computer records and spread sheets involving Thomas can't be accessed without my password, and he doesn't have it."

Harper turned to Gibson. "So anything he finds in the shared computer base will only show what we want the feds to see."

"Nothing but good news. I mean, I had to fudge our deposit accounts. They are on everyone's computer in the general ledger section. That's the only area where he may see a red flag, and that's easy enough to explain if we have to. We can tell him we had to cover some shortfalls from the condominium complex. Hell, Martin, tell him it was your money. He'll never know the source," Gibson urged.

"Good idea, Ronnie. If he hits me with any questions, that's what I'll tell him. That should hold him at bay."

"We better get over to the steps. The hearse is pulling up," Harper said.

Gibson took another puff and crushed the cigarette beneath his foot in the driveway. He followed his friend over to the front of the church. They stopped next to Senator Jim Murphy, who turned and automatically extended his hand.

"Good morning, Senator," Harper said as they clasped hands.

"Morning, Mr. Harper," Murphy said in a terse voice.

"This is my associate, Mr. Gibson."

The two men shook hands, but Murphy didn't speak. Then he turned back to the Harrington family, approaching John Harrington's widow and gave her a polite hug.

"Annabelle, my condolences to your family."

"Thank you, James. I know you were one of his very best friends. I appreciated your call the other night."

"That's the least I could do," Murphy said with a consoling tone.

He shook the hand of Harrington's college-age son and daughter and walked to the rear of the funeral car. Straining, Murphy and five other senators unloaded the casket over a curb and onto the gurney. The senator stepped to the side as the Bishop and two altar boys approached the casket for the blessing. After speaking briefly with the family the Bishop sprinkled holy water over the casket and read a passage from his hymnal.

Harper whispered into Gibson's ear, "Look at these hypocrites, acting like they are here to pay homage to Bubba. Truth is they are here because of protocol—that and the fear of pissing off Senator Murphy."

Chapter Nineteen

U.S. CUSTOMS OFFICE, PORT EVERGLADES FLORIDA - 10:15 AM

Osborne was sweating bullets as he paced the holding area for outgoing freight. He could see Guzman's BMW through the chain-link fence across the parking lot. Another customs agent came into the building and waved to Osborne from the other side. He waved back and acted like he was writing down information on a clipboard.

"Can you hear me? These guys are late," he shouted into the miniature microphone disguised as an American flag on his lapel.

"Chill out, Osborne," Guzman growled.

"They're always on time for any pickup. If you spooked them it's not going to be my fault they don't come in and pick up their merchandise."

"Don't get your shorts all knotted up," the agent said. "They'll be here. Just ease up and play it like you always do, and for God's sake, don't ask them why they were late."

"What if it goes bad? The only other guy who can help is at the far end of the building in a locked office. He won't be able to save my ass from these guys, and God only knows if you'll be able to get here in time," Osborne fretted.

"Don't worry. We have plenty of bodies inside and out of the building. They won't have time to grease you."

"You got somebody in this building? Are you nuts? You can't take them down here," a panicked Osborne screeched into the microphone.

"We're not going to take them down there. You're going to release their cargo, and we're going to follow them. Then your part of the deal is over, at least for now. I can see you with my binoculars, and so will they when they come around the corner of the building. So get off the airways and act busy. I'll give you a heads up when I see their car."

"What if they search me for a wire?" Osborne asked.

"That's not going to happen. Every federal employee in the country has a flag on their lapel just like you. The only difference is that yours is a high tech microphone. So don't turn your head to talk into it like you've been doing for the past five minutes and you'll be O.K. Trust me I can hear you loud and clear."

"All right," the customs agent sighed. He plopped down in his chair and checked out the manifest.

"It's show time, Osborne," the DEA agent warned. "Take a deep breath and think about the last time you got laid."

The powder blue Cadillac convertible pulled up the entry point. The driver handed a piece of paper to the guard, who checked his board, gave the signal to another guard inside, and the electronic gate rolled back. The dark-haired man behind the wheel waved his arm to the security guards then proceeded slowly until he reached building twelve.

He eased the car around the corner and stopped in front of a heavy metal gate.

Osborne hustled over to the front of the building and hit the button to raise the gate. Once they cleared the entry point he pressed the button again and the gate came silently down behind them. Both men got out of the convertible and walked toward the holding area.

Guzman took a rapid series of pictures of the two men through a telephoto lens. When he finished the roll of film he used his binoculars to follow the action.

"Grab that dolly and I'll take this one," Osborne said, pointing to the corner where a four-wheeled platform truck sat.

"Go get it, Pedro, and I'll sign the paper work," Batista said.

The driver began rolling the cart to the pickup area as Batista and Osborne looked over the paperwork. The Columbian signed the receipt for four olive-colored, heavy gauge steel containers. About the size of a large foot locker, each had reinforced steel corners and handles on both ends. They rested on a pair of plastic pallets.

"I can't believe you guys don't have a forklift to move this shit around with," Batista grumbled.

"We do, over in the other warehouse where they have bigger corrugated freight containers, like the ones you guys get in from Mexico. This warehouse is just for small stuff. That's why they give us freight dollies," Osborne explained.

Batista and Osborne grabbed an end of a container. The agent's palms were sweaty. He felt queasy, but he managed to heave it up a half a foot to the surface of the four-wheeled dolly with Batista's help.

"Damn, that's heavier than the last shipment," Osborne blurted out without thinking.

The Columbian frowned and gave Osborne a long look. The agent turned away and reached for the handle of the other container.

Batista went around the other side of the container and said, "You need more physical exercise and less dope, my friend." The Columbians cracked up.

"Everybody's a comedian," Osborne mumbled as they lifted the second container on the platform. Estacio, the driver, wheeled the dolly to the car and the Colombians loaded them into the back seat and covered them with a blanket. The trio returned and loaded the last two containers into the trunk.

"Open the gate. We're running late," Batista ordered, then turned to the agent. "Senor Osborne, I'll call you Tuesday and let you know when the next shipment is coming in. Stay out of trouble." He wagged his finger as he spoke.

"You know me."

"I do, that's why I told you to stay out of trouble."

"Yeah, yeah," Osborne grinned nervously. Hands trembling, he opened the gate and watched the car back out of the holding area.

"They're on their way," Osborne shouted. "Did you hear everything?"

"Loud and clear," Guzman said. "Don't do anything stupid like trying to bolt. Sit tight. My guy is on his way over to take you back to headquarters."

Guzman radioed his two partners. "The Caddy's on the way out. Keep a safe distance behind. I'll trail behind you guys far enough to alternate the tail using the cross streets. They may have a scanner, so use your cell to communicate with me."

As soon as he finished talking, he heard Osborne yelling back at him through the microphone, "I thought you said one of your guys was in the building?"

"Are you nuts? I wouldn't do that. Too dangerous for my guys. That's what listening devices are for. I wanted to give you a warm, fuzzy feeling so you'd think there was someone nearby to watch over you."

"You're a real bastard Guzman!"

"Tell me something I haven't heard before."

Chapter Twenty

WASHINGTON D.C. – 10:15 AM

Herzog picked up a couple of boxes of documents from Adrienne Boudreaux's office. He caught her as she was on her way out the door headed for the funeral. Even though he got to see her again, she didn't have a lot to say. She seemed miffed that he hadn't come by earlier, but he hoped she'd get over it.

When he got home he began poring over the documents. He separated the information into three sections—phone records, contributions and legislative information. With a sigh, he started with the phone records, underlining recurring numbers with a red Sharpie.

Two hours later he finished the initial look at the phone records. That left the grueling part, identifying the most frequent callers. That chore would go to Charlie Brune's assistant. It would take hours and his time would be better spent elsewhere.

The next order of business was the financial records, the campaign contributions in particular. The first file he opened was all the 527 campaign committees that Harrington was part of or received money from. The list contained both individual and corporate donors. He would compare these with individuals who contributed directly to Harrington's re-election campaign.

Once again he underlined the recurring names on the lists laid out across the table in his kitchen. He also underlined any amounts over the five-thousand-dollar level. When he finished that, he copied the names of all individual and corporate donors, where they were located, and the amounts they gave onto a legal pad.

He was surprised at the number of both types of contributors, not to mention the amounts they poured in. To him it was a glittering who's who of corporate banking. He suspected that many of the individual names he saw would also come up on the corporate side as well. But he wouldn't be able to confirm that until he cross-checked them with the 527 committee paperwork.

Herzog looked at the clock on the wall. He had been at it for four hours and was hungry. He slipped the stack of papers back into the file, went over to the refrigerator and opened the door. His wife would have been proud of him. Lots of fresh fruits and veggies, along with fresh ham and turkey for sandwiches. No fast food, leftovers, or pre-packaged food.

He made his favorite sandwich, roast turkey and provolone cheese, garnished with lettuce and mayo between two slices of salt-rye bread. He put that on a paper plate with a handful of salted cashews. Then he pulled out a frosted mug from the freezer and filled it with A&W Root Beer from a can. He tried to lick the foam before it poured over the top, but he wasn't fast enough.

"Damn, I would have thought by this time I'd have learned not to pour this too fast and get it all over the floor," he muttered in frustration.

Or in the alternative, he thought, he could have done what his wife always suggested, pour it over the sink. Then it wouldn't matter if it ran over. Funny, he thought, all the little memories of her that still went through his mind, even when he was thinking of something else. It had been two years since she died from injuries from the car wreck in Utah. Yet not a day went by that something she did or said didn't come back to him.

She had trained him well, even though he had been oblivious to it when it was occurring. Everything they were about was because of her. The way they raised their daughters, their lifestyle, their social life, their taste in food and wine—all of it was because of her.

She was smart, vibrant, outgoing, a beautiful person inside and out. He loved waking up every day with her by his side. They were partners in life, with her in the lead. She led and he followed. It was a simple, wonderful life, the stuff of dreams.

After her death the girls went off to college at Virginia Tech. Summer and long weekend visits with them were a cherished reminder of days past. He was still close to his daughters and talked with them every week, but it was not the same as having a complete family.

His work sustained him, but it was a poor substitute for the void that existed. He had been blessed with the kind of marriage that most people only dreamed about. It was the best. He never envisioned how bankrupt it would all become.

Time was the enemy. Filling the minutes and hours of the day with work and reading was his method of coping. At work by seven thirty and home by eight was the rule of thumb five days a week. Daily four-mile runs and keeping busy on the weekends became the prescription for his new life.

Days like today, when he fell asleep on the couch after lunch at three o'clock and didn't wake up until nine, with the house completely dark, were dramatic reminders of what his life had become. Now if only he could fall asleep and not be awake half the night, thinking about her, about them, and about the way life used to be.

Chapter Twenty-One

DEA OFFICE, MIAMI, FLORIDA – SUNDAY 8:00 AM

"Appreciate the update, your relief should be there in fifteen minutes. Keep your eyes open," Guzman said into his phone, then snapped it shut.

"Is that Davis and Rodriquez?" McPherson asked.

"Yeah, they're sitting on the warehouse where those two schleps dropped off the four containers. They'll return, and when they do we'll follow them. See where they take the shipment."

"You don't want to get a bead on them before they pick it up?" his boss asked.

"Nah, these guys are just little fish. I want the big kahuna."

"That makes sense," McPherson agreed.

"The customs agent doesn't know the contents of those containers, but said the turnaround is normally pretty quick. He didn't know where it was headed. That's why our guys are sticking around. We have no takers so far. If somebody doesn't come by today, I'm going back to the warehouse and put a bug on one of the containers. That way we can track it when they do pick it up. I'm going to need Jacobs to knock out their surveillance cameras while I do the dirty deed," Guzman told the head man.

"We never had this conversation," McPherson said. "Jacobs' phone number is in my rolodex. He'll be thrilled to get out in the field for a little action."

"Thanks, Chief."

"Is the customs agent back home?" McPherson asked.

"Yeah, I didn't want to put him in the lockup because I didn't know how soon we would need him again. Turns out they're going to call him again with information on another shipment. So we're going to have to let him keep his routine. I told him I'd be checking up on him randomly to make sure that he stays put. I have somebody watching the house. He's not going anywhere. I got a tap on his phone, too."

"Keep me posted if anything changes and you need some help. Why don't you go home and get some sleep," McPherson suggested.

"I am after I swing by Osborne's house and meet his wife on my way home. The three of us are going to have a little heart-to-heart talk. Just to make sure we're all on the same page."

McPherson's phone started ringing as Guzman got up from his desk and headed for the door.

Chapter Twenty-Two

SUNDAY-SIESTA KEY HARBOR - 11:00 AM

David Dreyer eased the white hulled, blue trimmed forty-foot cabin cruiser out of its slip at Siesta Key Marina and into the Inter-Coastal waterway that separated Siesta Key from the mainland. They floated quietly past villas with their private boat docks and screened in pools. Past the lush, green vegetation that cloaked the inland waterway. His wife Sarah was busy below deck, putting away snacks and stocking the refrigerator. His daughters, Chloe and Jennifer, were busy smearing suntan lotion on themselves.

Once they cleared the no wake zone Dreyer turned the boat north toward New Pass, their entry point into the Gulf of Mexico. The girls came up to the bridge in their deck shoes and walked to the bow of the boat. They spread their towels out on the smooth, flat section and stretched out.

"Make sure you have some thirty on your faces and noses," their father yelled.

"We already did that, Dad," Chloe answered.

Sarah came up from below wearing a two-piece, dark-blue bikini. The forty-year-old mother of two had blonde hair and a body that disguised her age. She was an exercise junkie who did her Pilates workout every day. Hair always done, makeup just so and designer clothes were just a part of what she was all about. So were her intellect and instincts about her husband.

David twisted around in the captain's chair and got a shot of the low-cut top and smiled as his eyes drifted to the Rio cut bottom. "You look sexy in that suit, dear."

"I'm glad I finally caught your attention. Is it too much skin?" his wife asked.

"Not from where I'm sitting. Did the girls say anything? They're your harshest fashion critics, you know."

"No, they didn't say a word. They couldn't wait to get up on deck and get some rays," she answered.

"That suit looks great on you. Why don't you come over here for awhile?" he motioned to her from his seat.

Sarah got up from her perch on the stern and sat in the captain's chair across from David. Dreyer steered the boat into the open channel, then headed north to Anna Marie Island. It was another sun-drenched day in Sarasota. The Sea Ray plied its way through the calm, blue-green waters of the Gulf. The glass-smooth water was broken periodically by dolphins surfacing in the distance.

Their weekly outings on the boat were something the whole family looked forward to, especially the teenage daughters who sometimes brought friends. This day it was family only. He planned to head north, anchor the boat near the shore and go diving in the shallow water. There would be fewer boats and less people than in the Sarasota.

Sarah bounced out of her chair and nestled up against her husband. "Hey mister, what's going on? You've been on another planet lately. Is it the job, me, the kids?" She shrugged her shoulders. "I don't remember the last time we made love. What's going on?"

"I'm sorry. I know I haven't been there for you lately. I can't tell you how bad I feel about almost being a no-show for Chloe's party. The other night when you tried to reach me at work and you couldn't get me on my cell phone there was a reason," he said in an ominous tone.

Sarah squeezed his hand and looked into his eyes, dreading his explanation.

"You're right, we need to talk. It's not about us, it's about what's going on at work," he said.

Sarah breathed a sigh of relief and gave him a quizzical look. Her intuition was that his issues could be related to something or someone else. "What's the problem? Daddy hasn't mentioned anything, other than asking if we were OK, because he saw the same things with you that I did."

"I'm going to tell you something, and it has to stay between us. This cannot get back to your father," he said as his eyes narrowed.

She nodded, and he continued. "The bank has a problem, and it involves our largest customer. That's as much as I can tell you now. Actually, the less you know, the better it will be for everyone. That's what's been bothering me lately. "

"You're scaring me, David. Who else is in trouble—you, my dad, Ronnie?"

"I can't tell you any more right now, other than I'm not involved. That's why you can't talk to anyone about this, especially your dad. After all the dust settles I may not have a job, but I'm definitely not part of the problem."

"Oh my God, is the bank going under?" Sarah asked.

"I don't know, but I can guarantee you that the feds will be involved. Depending on what they find, they may or may not revoke its charter. Either way, my life as head of commercial lending and retail is over," he asserted.

A tear rolled down her cheek. She turned her head away and wiped it just as Chloe walked around the side of the cabin.

"Jen and I need something to drink. We're just baking out there. Do you guys want something?"

"Yeah, while you're down there could you bring us a couple of bottles of water?" her father asked.

"Sure, Dad."

Chloe went below and Sarah tried to regain her composure. She took a couple of steps down to the bench seat on the stern and grabbed a towel. Then she came back up to the captain's chair. Chloe bounded up the steps and handed her a couple of bottles of mineral water. "Thanks. Are you guys good up there, or do you want some snacks?" Sarah asked

"No thanks, mom, we're good. How much longer until we get to Anna Marie Island Daddy?"

He glanced at his watch. "At least another twenty minutes."

"Good, that means we get a half hour of sun on each side," the teenager said.

Chloe stepped between the railing and the cabin and returned to her perch on the bow. Sarah sat back down in her chair and took a drink of water.

"What are we going to do, David?"

"This is my problem to deal with," he declared. "You can't be involved. I'm in the process of figuring out who I need to talk to and when."

"We're going over to my parent's house tonight for dinner. How can I sit there and act like nothing is going on?" she questioned.

Dreyer took his hand off the wheel and gently touched Sarah's shoulders. "Hon, you have no choice. You have to do this. Talk about the kids, our vacation next month. Just be upbeat. No matter what happens at the bank we're going to survive."

Sarah dabbed at her cheek with the towel and Dreyer put his hands back on the wheel.

"Look, our house and cars are paid for. We have a pretty good chunk of cash in the bank and a nice stock portfolio. The only thing we owe money on is this boat. We have enough to live on our savings for a while. If need be I can probably get a job consulting. So don't hit the panic button yet. We're going to be all right."

He put his arm around her and she buried her head in his shoulder and sobbed, "I can't believe this is happening to us. We have the perfect life. Now you tell me it's all going to change, and I shouldn't be upset. I don't know if I can do this," she said tearfully.

"Then call your parents house right now," Dreyer told her as he handed her his cell phone. "Tell them we can't make it for dinner and give them some excuse."

"But if what you are saying is true then Daddy will be even more suspicious if we miss dinner with them."

"Sarah, you are making my point for me. That is exactly the reason you have to act normal. Like we hit a little bump in the road, like a lot of couples do. Gloss it all over. You're smart and convincing. You can pull that off," he told her.

"I guess I don't have any choice, do I?" Sarah said reluctantly.

"Not really."

Chapter Twenty-Three

SARASOTA, FLORIDA - 12:00 NOON

The drive back from mass at St. Michael's Catholic Church at the north end of Siesta Key took about five minutes. The navy blue Mercedes E-class sedan they were riding in was Thomas Vasquez' pride and joy. That and his forty-five year old trophy wife Elena, an ex-model and former Miss Columbia. She was a tall, slender woman with olive complexion, high cheekbones and raven-colored shoulder length hair, a classic Latin beauty.

He loved her and felt like he was king of the world whenever people saw him with her. Being with both at the same time was a bonus for him. As the car turned left onto Midnight Pass Road his cell phone rang.

"Hello... Where are you calling me from? I'm almost home. Let me call you back on the land line. Give me the number."

Elena reached in her purse and handed him a pocket-size notebook and pen. He scribbled the number down and hung up. "Thank you, dear."

"I didn't want to see you have an accident with your baby while you tried to find something to write with," she teased.

"You're always looking out for me," he said as he reached over and playfully squeezed her hand.

He turned the car into the Palm Island Club entry lane and drove slowly past the administration building and swimming pool. He took the last parking spot under the canopy facing the rear of the building. They got out and rode the elevator to the tenth floor. After a short walk to the end of the hall he opened the door for Elena.

The walls of the condo were floor to ceiling glass except for the stuccoed corners of the room. The bedrooms and the kitchen faced out toward the translucent water of the Gulf of Mexico with decks off both rooms. The living room and dinning area afforded a spectacular southern exposure of Crescent Beach. They had an unobstructed two-mile view all the way down to the point of rocks at the end of the beach.

Elena walked into the bedroom and started to undress. Vasquez picked the phone up off of the white wicker table and stood by the window as he punched in the numbers.

"Hello, Tomas?"

"Yes Carlos, I'm glad you called me from a pay phone. Were there any problems yesterday at customs?"

"No, our guy was there to meet us and it went without a hitch. The containers are stashed in the warehouse. We're going to drive up tomorrow like we planned and meet you tomorrow night," Batista told him.

"There's been a slight change in plans. I still want you to bring the container up tomorrow, but I can't meet you until at least nine o'clock. I forgot to tell you last week when we planned this that I have a soccer game with the kids from church. I have to be there. Stay on the same schedule and bring the shipment up. When you get here take it to the storage locker we used before."

"OK boss, that won't be a problem."

You'll have to kill some time. So why don't you get some dinner at Selva Grille on Main Street and I'll meet you there later. About nine o'clock," Vasquez told his man.

"See you tomorrow night boss."

"Be careful Carlos."

He hung the phone up and headed for the bedroom. His wife was wearing a new two-piece red swimsuit with gold trim that showed off every curve of her body.

"Would you fasten the clip on the back dear?"

"This suit looks like it was designed for your body the way it fits so perfectly. It does not leave much to the imagination though," he said as he hooked the gold clasp on the back of her suit. He frowned.

"Everything is covered. I'm not indecent, just sexy," Elena purred.

Vasquez put his hand on both shoulders, turned her around and kissed her.

"What was that for darling?"

"For being you. I love you," he told her as he brought her closer to him.

"You are so sweet Tomas."

"I'll change into my suit and be ready in a second. Can you get the drinks and the cooler ready while I'm changing?" he asked.

"I can do that. Do you want me to throw in some salty snacks and fruit?"

"That would be great," he said.

Five minutes later they were walking out of the building in their flip flops and onto the cool, sugary sands of Siesta Key Beach. He sat their cooler and bag on a lounge chair next to their rainbow colored beach umbrella. "Which way up or down?"

"Let's go down toward the point of rocks and see how we feel when we get back. It's not too hot today. It's a good day for us to get our exercise. If we're not too tired maybe we can go up to the public beach."

"You're the boss Elena."

They went south on the beach hand in hand, a pair of suntanned beach combers, thin and tall with their matching black hair. As they strolled along the sands the midday tide gently lapped at their feet. With his beautiful wife at his side he was on top of the world. He was at the place in his life where he always hoped he would be.

This was worlds away, both literally and figuratively, from the life he led in war-torn Columbia. He had not only made it out, he had gone from being moderately successful in South America to being rich in the States.

His friends in the drug cartel were the source of the seed money used to build his financial empire. But it was his investments in real estate and his hard work that got him where he was today.

Elena had been with him through it all but was never involved in the seamy side of his business affairs. That was by design and fine by her. She knew what her husband did but never moralized about it. The only facet of his business she was involved in was their real estate portfolio.

Their safety net was their large cash position in their account located on Grand Turk Island. They made frequent trips down there in his Cessna Citation jet making deposits and withdrawals of large sums of cash, depending on their needs.

All the rest of their assets, other than their estate in Cartagena, were in the United States and Switzerland. He was prepared to do whatever was necessary to protect himself and his wife. As an ex-military official and consular officer, he had done many things, including killing people, to get what he needed. He was prepared to do it again if the situation warranted.

Chapter Twenty-Four

SARASOTA AIRPORT - 1:00 PM

Kevin Henry taxied the Gulfstream over to the hangar. Ronnie Gibson was at the exit door. He pressed the switch, unlocked the door and the steps folded down. Martin Harper was just about to go down when he turned to the pilot and asked, "Are you available for golf on Tuesday morning? We're over at Longboat Key."

"Yeah, I don't have anything going Tuesday except hitting the beach sometime. Thanks for the invitation, Mr. Harper. I'd like to play at Longboat again with you."

"Good, I'll try and get David to play and if that doesn't work out we'll pick up a couple of guys from the club to round out our foursome. Always plenty of guys over there looking for a game. We'll figure out whether we're going to play five-buck Nassau after we see how our third or fourth player hits the ball on the driving range," Harper said.

"Great. See you Tuesday," the pilot confirmed to the banker.

When the conversation was finished Harper left the Gulfstream and made a beeline for his

Corvette. The pilot glanced at him, then stepped back into the cockpit and finished his paperwork for the FAA. His co-pilot was throwing the food from the cabin into a plastic trash bag. A cleaning crew would come in later and clean the entire cabin, but it was part of the routine that both pilots followed. One cleaned up the food right after the flight while the other finished the paperwork. Harper owned this jewel, but they treated it like it was theirs.

Kevin never looked at this facet of his job as demeaning. He considered the plane his office and he wanted everything letter perfect. His attitude came from his training at the Air Force Academy and the ten years he flew as a commercial pilot for Delta.

He was all business when he flew and used his free time to play golf, go to the beach and track his investments. The pilot was a scratch golfer who got to play with his boss at least once a month at Sarasota's finest courses. The best part was that it was an all day comp for him, and more times than not he came away with a couple hundred bucks in his pocket from the five dollar Nassau and side bets everybody made.

A six figure income, a yellow Dodge Viper and a beach condo were the staples of his life. His current love, a thirty-five year old attorney, who had just moved in with him was the only possible threat to his confirmed bachelor status.

At forty years old his life was one that he had planned for and achieved. He was just one of many snow birds who relocated to Florida. Once there he took advantage of the laid back beach lifestyle. It took money to live that way, but he was well compensated. His job and his investments gave him the ability to live the lifestyle that he enjoyed so much.

The product of a conservative family, his value system was never challenged before he made the move to Florida and became Harper's corporate pilot.

But once Harper was named ambassador to Switzerland things changed.

They were never there more than a couple of days, he never took his wife and he always seemed anxious. After awhile Henry's curiosity got the best of him. Waiting inside a hangar at the Zurich airport on a rainy, steel gray afternoon last March, his worst fears were confirmed. Harper came back to the aircraft and unloaded an unusual amount of luggage into a limousine.

He observed the same thing with Harper on successive trips. The plane was always loaded prior to his arrival and unloaded after his departure, so he never had the opportunity to check out the contents in the cargo hold. Henry and his co-pilot were always the last to load luggage. It was hard to determine exactly how many items were back there or what was inside any of them. But the hold was always filled on the trip out and nearly empty on the return.

The passenger suitcases never went through customs, a diplomatic perk that was obviously being abused. Kevin tried to keep it out of his mind, but the suspicion that he was participating in something illegal gnawed at him. In fact, he didn't know for sure what was inside the luggage. From a legal standpoint as long as he didn't know the contents he was not a willing participant.

Still, he couldn't reconcile the notion that he was an enabler. He was ex-military, having served his country in the first Gulf War. The little voice in his head told him that no matter what the contents of the suitcases were, what he was doing wasn't kosher. It had to be either money or drugs, and both came from the same source.

He couldn't keep a blind eye to what was going on indefinitely, but he had to have some hard evidence before he went to the authorities. There was only one way to satisfy his curiosity: check out the luggage after it was loaded in Sarasota and before they flew out to Zurich.

When that time came, he would need Paul's help and he knew that he could count on him. When to pull the trigger was the issue that kept resurfacing. Kevin and Paul were dependent upon one another and knew each other's backgrounds pretty well. The only relevant information Kevin held back was his relationship with Harper's girlfriend, Sherry. They had been an item when Kevin was flying for Delta out of Cincinnati. After a couple of years they broke it off by mutual agreement. He hadn't had any contact with her until his boss brought her on board the plane a couple of years ago on a flight from Cincinnati to the Bahamas.

It was an awkward reunion that both pulled off without Harper being any the wiser to their past. Doing that gave him the confidence to carry out the charade as a clueless pilot.

The juggling act between business associate and investigator wasn't something he relished. But the mysterious suitcases were something he was going to have to confront sooner, rather than later.

Chapter Twenty-Five

SARASOTA - 7:00 PM

David Dreyer pulled the car into the circular, paver stone driveway at Martin Harper's University Park home. The kids bounded out of the back seat and hugged their grandmother and grandfather as they met them in the driveway.

"How was the water today?" their grandfather asked.

"It was great, Grandpa. I wish you and Grandma could have come along with us," Chloe told him as they followed them to the front door.

"That would have been nice, hon. Did you get a chance to relax today, David?" Harper said, trying to get a read on his son-in-law.

"As a matter of fact I did, Martin. When did you guys get back?"

"Early this afternoon. We wanted to get out last night, but we couldn't. We had to talk to some people before we left Washington. Otherwise we would have been home earlier."

He paused and turned as they approached the door to the house. "Oh, before I forget, I scheduled golf over at Longboat Key Club for

Tuesday. Check your calendar. I'd like you to go if you can. I asked Kevin to play, and we can get a fourth from one of the members."

"I appreciate the invitation, but with the audit and everything else going on I don't think I'll be able to make it. But I really appreciate the offer. I love playing over there. Can I take a rain check?"

"Absolutely, we can do it some other time," Harper promised.

"That would be great. Thanks."

Dreyer followed the rest of the family into the house. The marble floor entry foyer extended past the living room on the left and the master bedroom on the right. The great room and dinning area were just beyond the kitchen. The soft yellow interior walls gave way to a bank of windows and doors that led to the swimming pool and screened in lanai. The rear of the property was bordered by a lake some thirty feet past the swimming pool.

Judith Harper, Marvin's wife, carried out wine for the adults and soft drinks for the kids. They relaxed around the pool in lounge chairs talking with each other like any other family. The primary topic of conversation centered on the girls and their impending soccer camp trip.

Judith served a gourmet dinner on the patio, and David became more involved in the conversation as the meal progressed. He was guarded in what he said, masking his concern for the impending implosion at the bank. But he put on a real dog and pony show, laughing at some of the girls' remarks, even asking for a second glass of Pinot Noir before he finished his salmon.

Sarah squeezed his hand under the table. Her way of telling him how appreciative she was of his behavior. She was relieved that their visit had gone so well, despite what he had told her earlier. David was also relieved that she didn't act strange or withdrawn. He played off her act, which didn't allow Harper any chance to read anything into their behavior.

When it was time to leave, everybody was smiling and making small talk as they walked to the front door.

"Judith, thanks for having us over. Dinner was lights out, as always," Dreyer said as he hugged her.

"Thank you, David. I'm glad you were able to make it over. I love our Sunday get togethers."

"Thanks Daddy, thanks Mom," Sarah said as she hugged her father, then her mother.

The girls gave their grandparents goodbye hugs, and the family walked a couple steps down to the car.

"See you tomorrow at the office," Martin waved.

"I'll be there bright and early," Dreyer said forcing a smile. "I have some loans that I'm closing on tomorrow and I have to check over the documents."

"Love those loan closings, instant cash for the bank," Harper said with a smile on his face."

"Enough of the shop talk you guys," Sarah said as she opened the door to the car. "Love you, good night."

"Good night dear, good night girls," Judith said as they waved goodbye, watching the green Lexus pull out of the circular palm lined driveway.

Chapter Twenty-Six

NAPLES, FLORIDA – MONDAY 8:00 AM

"Are you still getting a good signal from the tracking device on your screen?" Guzman shouted over his radio to the lead chase car.

"Affirmative, but I've lost a visual on them. The rain's too heavy and I'm too far behind them," his man Davis responded.

"You guys are still in good shape. I can see both of your cars on my screen. They're still headed north," Guzman told him.

The rain was pelting his car horizontally as Guzman drove north on Interstate 75. He was barely able to see the city limits sign for Naples. After hydroplaning a couple of times trying to catch up to his men Guzman eased off the gas and slowed down.

"What's your location," the lead agent asked.

"We passed the 107 mile marker a couple of minutes ago," Davis answered.

"Good, I'm coming up on it right now. Dammit! The van you're chasing stopped. I can't tell exactly how far in front of you they are, but they have to be right by the side of the road. Do you see anything?"

"No, but we're coming up on an exit at the 111 mile marker. There's some gas stations up ahead. Should we take the exit?" Davis called back.

"No, keep going. I'll jump off at the 111-mile marker and check it out," Guzman told the team.

"We'll keep heading north until we hear otherwise. Shit, I must have missed them when they pulled over. I was too busy looking for a mile marker. I can't see anything with this damn storm," the agent told his boss.

"Davis, they are stationary, to the east of you. They must have exited at 111. What's your location?"

"Approaching the 116-mile marker, just south of Bonita Springs."

"Pull off to the side of the road while I check this out for a minute."

Guzman looked at his monitor for a couple of minutes and called back to Davis.

"They're on the move again, approaching from the east. Do you see them on your screen?"

"No, we aren't picking anything up," Davis answered.

"They're approaching your position. The vehicle just turned west. They have to be headed over to 41. Get over there as fast as you can."

"We're on 75 at the sign for Bonita Springs. We'll take the 116 exit and head toward 41, but I don't see the damn white van," the frustrated agent shouted in the mic.

"They're still in front, but I can't tell you how far. Stay on them. We can't lose them again. I'm two miles south of the Bonita Springs exit," Guzman told them as he looked at the tracking monitor. "Can you see them?"

"No, we're on 41 and passing everybody, but we still haven't spotted them," Davis reported.

There was a long pause that followed. "Ah shit, that isn't good."

"What's going on," Guzman demanded.

"We're at the city limits of Bonita Springs, stopped for a traffic light. They have to be in the same mess we are. The traffic ahead is all stop and go. We'll just keep going."

"We got a problem. I've got nothing on my screen. Shit! Pull over to the side of the highway."

After ranting, raving and banging the tracking screen, Guzman pulled over. Another couple of minutes passed before his screen came back on.

"We're back in business. They changed directions and are going north," Guzman said. "I'm a couple of miles back. Keep going north until I tell you otherwise."

Guzman passed Daniels Parkway, the major east-west artery of the town and the rain began to ease up.

"They're still going north. What's your location?" the lead agent asked.

"Still on 41, approaching College Parkway."

"Keep going. I'll be able to catch up now with the rain slowing down."

Guzman sped up and a couple of minutes later he rolled up along side his agents. "Let's move up in tandem. They are literally right ahead of us. According to my screen they are just in front of the semi on the right lane. They are exiting off the highway. I'll drop in behind you."

The agents caught a glimpse of a panel van turning right off 41. A quarter of a mile later they pulled into a Shell station. The rain picked up again and they couldn't see ten feet in front of them. They left their headlights on and waited for Guzman as they pulled into the station.

The white panel van was under the canopy at the far end of the island, some fifty feet away. A minute later Guzman pulled up alongside them and lowered his window. "Is it the van at the last set of pumps?"

"That's it," Rodriquez said.

"That van doesn't look right," Guzman said.

"It is definitely the one that pulled in here."

"Anybody get out and go inside the store?" Guzman asked.

"The driver, there he is, walking back to the pump."

"Let him finish filling the tank. You pull up to the pump behind him and I'll wait until he finishes, then block him in."

Rodriquez rolled up behind the van and stepped out of the car. Davis had slid down in the seat to avoid being seen while the other agent acted like he was searching for his credit card in his wallet. As soon as the man was finished filling the van and put the pump back, Guzman zipped in front of the truck.

"Go!" Rodriquez yelled to Davis.

The agent slid out of the seat and ran to the passenger side door of the van with his gun drawn.

Guzman ran up to the driver.

"DEA. Put your hands above your head and spread eagle across the front of the van."

At the same time Davis swung open the passenger side door.

"DEA!" he screamed. "Get out of the van and on the ground."

He yanked out a light skinned guy wearing a white painter's suit.

"We got a problem," Rodriquez yelled as he slammed the back door closed and walked to the front of the van. "There's no containers in this van, but our tracking device is."

"Don't move," Guzman warned. "Davis, bring the other guy over here and keep an eye on them."

Guzman hopped around to the rear of the van and swung the door open. "Son-of-a-bitch! What the hell happened? Let's see what these guys have to say. I knew this van didn't look right as soon as I pulled in," the lead agent swore.

They walked back to the front of the truck. Guzman put his nine millimeter back in his holster. "You two guys turn around and keep your hands above your head. Davis, keep your weapon on them while I talk to them."

"All right, tell me how you got our GPS tracking device in the rear of your van," Guzman said as he scanned the suspect's driver's license.

"I'm sorry sir. I don't know what you're talking about. The only stop we made since we left home this morning was for coffee over at the BP station outside Naples. We have a painting job at a beach-side home just up the road. The address is in the front of the truck on my work order. Check it out. I don't know who you are looking for, but we're painters."

"Check it out, Rodriquez."

"He's got a work order, all right. And the van has a half-dozen five-gallon buckets of paint and tarps. Ask him the name of the guy he works for."

"I work for Rusty Schuckmann. My name is Darrell and he's Jesse."

Rodriquez threw his palms up. Guzman rolled his head back and blew out a hard shot of air. "We just wasted the whole morning chasing after a couple of painters. Great!"

He looked at the two men whose mouths were still agape and told them, "All right, you guys can lower your hands. I'm sorry we jumped your case, but your van looked like the guys we've been following since early this morning. Tell me what happened when you went in to get coffee. Did both of you guys go in at the same time?"

"Yeah, we did. Jesse went in to use the head and I got the coffee for us. I made sure I could see the truck from inside. You know you just cain't trust anybody any more. Wasn't like there was anything to steal 'cept our boom box and the paint for the job. Hail, we didn't even lock it up."

"Darrell, did you happen to see another van like yours or notice anybody acting strange?"

"You know, there was this dude in front of me at the register cussing at the clerk," the painter told him.

"About what?" Guzman frowned.

"Cuz the clerk told him he couldn't make change fur a fifty dollar bill that he gave him for a couple of bottles of water. This guy was ma-ad. I mean he storms out then comes back and throws a ten dollar bill in the man's face. I couldn't believe ma eyes."

"Can you describe this guy?" Guzman prodded.

"Yes sir. He had one of those heavy Spanish accents, and the man was dripping with jewels, gold everywhere."

"And don't forget Darrell, he was in a white suit and dark blue shirt," the other painter reminded him.

"Yeah, that's right. Then this gah walks out and goes around our van. A scoche later I see a white van, just like Jesse's and mine, peel out of the station. Must have been his. Ours was parked by the front set of pumps. Didn't notice his when we'd rode up in all the rain. Musta been there when we pulled up, but I never saw it."

"What did this guy look like?" the lead agent wanted to know.

"Fella was about as big as me. Had that dark, shiny black hair, blue shirt, and white trousers. Had a tattoo of a snake on his neck. I mean this dude looked real mean. Ain't nobody I'd wanta tango with. Know what I mean?"

Rodriquez and Davis bit their lips and had to look away.

"How long were you in there?" Guzman asked.

"Don't know for sure, wada you think Jesse, five minutes?"

"I'd say."

"Hadda wait for the guy to refill the coffee machine. Then we paid and left."

"Thanks guys. You've been a big help. Sorry about the hassle. Hope we didn't screw your day up too bad," Guzman said as he sauntered back to his car.

"Ain't goin to be a problem agent. Whenever Jessie and I git there, we git there."

Guzman pulled his car up far enough for them to pull out and the painters waved to him as they left the station.

"I don't know how the perps found the bug, but they did. They must have thrown it in the painter's truck while Darrell and his buddy were inside." Guzman fumed. "We're back to square one. Who knows where they are by now?"

"What about an alert to the locals?" Rodriguez suggested.

"Why not at this point? We're screwed, blued and tattooed. Go ahead and have the locals issue an APB for the van, even though they probably ditched it by now. With all this damn rain chances are nobody will see it anyway. What the hell, go ahead and call Naples and Ft Myers PD. Nothing to lose at this point."

Guzman tossed the tracking device in the car. "I'll call the office and make sure our informant gets moved. This guy might figure Osborne fingered him. Shit, we're back to square one."

Chapter Twenty-Seven

WASHINGTON D.C., MONDAY - 9:00 AM

"Good morning. Would either of you guys like some coffee or pastries? There are some of both on the table," the Chief told his men.

"Thanks Charlie, I didn't have time to stop this morning," Trupp said as he reached for a cup of coffee, then a Danish.

Herzog did the same and went back to his chair after laying a couple of computer sheets out on the desk.

"What are these?" Brune asked.

"They're the most frequent phone contacts Harrington had. I figured your assistant could run them down faster than I could," Herzog told him as he took a bite of his roll.

"Yeah, you're right, better her than you."

"Thank God for Starbucks. How did the world survive before them?" Trupp declared as he finished his roll and took a sip of coffee.

Brune opened a manila folder on his desk. "I ran the name of Carlos Batista through the computer and he wasn't in our data base. So I gave Metro-Dade a call. Our boy was arrested a year ago for assault and battery in Miami. The charges were dismissed when the witness failed to appear at the hearing. I spoke with the detective in charge of the case. Turns out the guy he assaulted is officially listed as a missing person and Batista's in the wind. They don't have a clue where he is."

"Really?" Trupp said as he lowered his cup of coffee from his lips.

"What's his background?" Herzog asked.

"He used to live in the Coconut Grove section of Miami, not exactly the low rent district."

"Any work history?" Trupp inquired.

"You guys will love this," Brune said dryly. "He listed his source of income as an export-import consultant. That would be OK, except that he doesn't list any address for a place of business. Just his home phone, which of course is disconnected."

"Can we get a search warrant to see who he's talked with in the past?" Herzog fired back.

"I've already applied for it and should have it before noon. I'll have the Miami office execute it for us."

"Anything that caught your eye in the financial reports Rich?"

"Yeah. One name kept popping up on both the individual and corporate 527 contribution lists."

"Really? Who is it?"

"Martin Harper, president of Gulfcoast Bank."

Brune's eyebrows rose. "How far back does the relationship go?"

"At least six years. Two companies and one individual led the parade for the past six years, giving tons of money."

"Start with the 527 committees because they're usually bigger," Brune said.

"Friends of Harrington raised a little over a million per year. Martin Harper, president of Gulf coast Bank, was the biggest single contributor. The next largest corporate contributor was a company called Caribbean Ventures, which interestingly enough, is a subsidiary of a Panamanian holding company called New Horizons. The rest of the contributor's list is a who's who of the National Banking Association. Gulfcoast Bank was by far the largest corporate contributor to John Harrington the past two years, giving him $200,000 per year."

"Where are the companies located?"

"Both of these firms are located in Sarasota," Herzog told Brune.

"Correct me if I'm wrong, but isn't Harper the current ambassador to Switzerland?" Trupp asked.

"He most certainly is," Brune affirmed, as the light came on for everybody at the same time.

"So these guys were in bed together. I'd love to know what Harrington had to do for them to contribute that much money?" Trupp wondered.

"I'm in the process of finding out," Herzog replied. "I'm going over to Harrington's office and pick up the legislative information for the past six terms from Ms. Boudreaux. I didn't get much from his travel itinerary, lunch meetings or his junkets. But maybe I can connect the dots when I go over his legislative records."

"That's the next piece of the puzzle and that may take awhile to decipher," Herzog continued. "But I'll figure it out. The only other thing that rang my bell was that these guys also gave some pretty big bucks to Senator Murphy's campaign and Harper also headed one of his 527 committees."

"Damn, these boys covered all their bases," Brune said as he sat back in his chair.

"Russ, have your guys wrapped up the forensic part of the investigation?"

"Not yet. We're still looking for the killer's DNA in the Escalade. Harrington's blood matches the sample taken from inside the Honda, which by the way was stolen the night of the murders. We have the blood spatters and the DNA from outside the shooter's car, but we didn't get any prints off the shell casings outside the victim's car. All we have is a fuzzy picture of him leaving the hotel parking lot. It may or may not be Batista."

"Keep processing the crime scene and the car," Brune said. "Maybe something will turn up. I'm having trouble making the connection between the killer, if it is Batista, and Harrington. We'll have to see where the information leads us. Even if we were able to find Batista and pick him up, at this point I wouldn't want to prosecute this case with circumstantial evidence. And that's all we have right now."

"Should one of us go down to south Florida to check this guy out?" Trupp asked.

"Probably at some point, but not right now. I'm going to call the FBI office in Miami and see if they can dig up any more information on Batista. You guys keep working the case from here and let's see where things lead us. Any issues with your chief, Russ?"

"No, he's a happy camper since you sent him some money to cover the costs for the forensic staff overtime. He made a special point this morning to swing by and make sure I conveyed his thanks to you."

"Give my best to Mickey," the senior investigator said.

"Trust me, he's no fan of the Washington press corp. He's thrilled you decided to handle this. He hates the media, calls them vermin and parasites, a bunch of self-serving bastards."

"That's why we always got along so well. Great minds think alike."

"I don't know how you can talk to the press every day and answer the same asinine questions," Trupp said as he finished his coffee.

"I want them to think we are clueless, and that allows them to use their thimble-sized brains to speculate and manufacture bullshit. Then they come to me for confirmation and I get to show everybody how incredibly shallow they really are. It's actually fun. I treat them like mushrooms, keep them in the dark and feed them shit. It allows you guys to do your work without them having a clue as to what's really going on," Brune said.

"I have to get out of here and see Ms. Boudreaux," Herzog said. "Unless you want me back here later, I'm going home to sort through the legislative information."

"No, that's fine, see you tomorrow."

"Russ, did anything turn up at the girlfriend's apartment, or in her background?" Brune asked.

"Nah, we drew a blank. She had recently broken up with her boyfriend back in Richmond, but he checked out. A dead end, whatever we have is sitting in front of us. We just have to sort it out. We've canvassed every hotel and motel within ten miles of the crime scene, nothing there either."

"What about the vehicle?"

"The killer boosted the car from a Georgetown medical student. We didn't get the robbery report until the day after the murder. He was an intern. Didn't know it was missing for two days."

"Rich is going to check out the women Harrington has been with in the last few years to see if anything jumps out," Brune said. "But I'm not holding my breath."

"Yeah, I agree that's a long shot."

"I'll have my FBI contact do a thorough investigation of Batista. They'll do INS, State Department, military and DEA background checks on him," their boss promised.

"This guy Batista is no Boy Scout. As crowded as the jails are in Miami he could have pleaded that out as a misdemeanor, with no jail time and a maximum hundred dollar fine. So it looks like he greased the guy instead," Trupp said.

"That's how the lead detective reads it too. He said they'll keep a lookout for him. Maybe we'll get lucky and this guy will surface again."

Trupp got up from his chair and grabbed his brief case. "I'm going to pound the bricks up in Georgetown, see if anybody saw him. He had to stay somewhere. We went back and checked his flight itinerary. He arrived three days before Harrington was murdered."

"Did you check the motels near the Georgetown campus?" Brune wanted to know.

"Not yet, but that's our next stop. Georgetown is where he boosted the car, so he probably was familiar with the area. All we know for sure right now is that he dumped the car across the river and took the subway. We'll keep on working it."

"Sounds good, I'll give you a call if we get any more information from Miami."

Chapter Twenty-Eight

SENATOR HARRINGTON'S OFFICE - 11:00 AM

"I appreciate your being so punctual Richard," Adrienne Boudreaux said as her assistant led the agent into the office. "Caroline, please close the door on your way out."

"Yes, Ms. Boudreaux," her secretary said as she closed the door behind her.

She turned to Herzog. "Would you care for some coffee?'

"No, thank you," Herzog replied.

"I hope you had a good weekend. Mine was dreadful, with the senator's funeral and all the upheaval we're going through here."

Herzog sat passively as she rambled on for a few minutes about the problems of keeping the office staff intact and her work. Then she stopped on the dime and asked, "Would you care to join me for lunch at the Four Seasons? We can go over the legislative information and I can also identify some women he dated in the past year."

"Uh-sure. But I'm on a tight schedule," Herzog answered. The invitation had taken him by surprise. He wasn't used to a woman being this up front.

"Let me grab my jacket and we'll be on our way."

"Parking is going to be a little tight at this time of day, isn't it?" Herzog asked.

"Not an issue. I know the parking valet. Neither the senator nor I ever had a problem getting in or out of there."

"You are full of surprises, Adrienne."

The pair left the office and proceeded down to the lower level garage. Herzog scrambled around and opened the passenger side door. She put the files on the backseat of his car and he hustled around to the driver's side.

The sunlight hit them like a laser when they got to street level. Herzog pulled the visor down and turned right onto Pennsylvania Avenue. They arrived at the hotel ten minutes later. The valet swung the door open and Adrienne stepped out and offered her hand to him.

"Ms. Boudreaux, I was shocked to hear about Senator Harrington," the valet told her as he shook her hand.

"Thank you Marcus, we all miss him very dearly."

"Well it's nice to see you again and don't worry about the car. I'll have it waiting for you right here when you come out."

She gave him a twenty and walked past the bellman to the entrance.

Herzog went back and grabbed the files off the seat while she waited inside the entrance. They went through a second set of glass doors to the hostess station. The maitre de recognized her and came over. He spoke briefly to the hostess, motioned to them to follow him, and escorted them to a circular booth at the rear of the room. They had a booth with a view of both the bar and the dining area. Adrienne thanked him and he smiled back appreciatively.

"Let me guess Adrienne, this is your table?"

"Very good Richard. Now, eyes left. Check out the tall blonde at the next table with the two glasses of wine on her tray. She is definitely one of the senator's ex-lovers. And so is the dark-haired waitress at the table for four, over to our right."

Herzog swiveled his head and asked, "Adrienne, how do you know for sure?"

"Because the senator got drunk one night when we were here and boasted about his exploits. He could be a real bastard—and let me assure you, he was definitely not a gentleman. He was nothing more than an educated, rich, good ole boy. I always felt sorry for his wife."

Herzog paused for a moment not sure what to say. He said the first thing that came to his mind. "That sounds strange coming from you."

A pained expression came across Adrienne's face.

"Richard, hindsight is always twenty-ten. It was one of the biggest mistakes of my life. It was just a fling for him. He used me just like he used those waitresses, his neighbor, his real estate agent and everyone else. I genuinely cared for him and thought I could handle it," she said as she pulled out a kerchief.

The dark haired waitress that she had pointed out earlier came over to the table, handed them menus, and told them what the luncheon special was. After taking their drink order for two glasses of Chardonnay, she left.

"I'm sorry Adrienne, I apologize for my remark," he said. Then he scooted closer to her and touched her hand.

"Look, we don't have to stay here. I have the files with the other women's names and addresses. If this is too much we can leave."

"That's very kind of you, but I'm all right. I didn't think coming back to this place would dredge up all those old feelings. Having said that, we needed to come here so that you could get information on some of the women I knew about."

Lunch lasted another hour and a half and a bottle of Chardonnay. Both were oblivious to the time. They talked non-stop during and after the meal. It was the first time Herzog had been out of his house for a social occasion since his wife died two years ago He was enjoying himself and not feeling the least guilty about it.

By the time lunch was over whatever preconceived notion he had about Adrienne Boudreaux's personal life had been removed. Beneath her steely, formal veneer, was a caring, vulnerable person. Someone who helped him more than she knew.

What started out as a day he dreaded had inexplicably turned 180 degrees for him.

Chapter Twenty-Nine

GULFCOAST BANK - 1:00 PM

"Ronnie, we'll be getting another shipment in," Harper informed his heavy set partner. "I just got off of the phone with Thomas."

"Good thing, because as it turned out we didn't have enough cash. What's the holdup with Thomas getting the money over to us? I thought it was supposed to be here late this afternoon." Gibson took a drink of Coke, burped and set the can back down on his desk.

"He said something about getting a late start and not getting here until later this evening."

Gibson took another gulp and shrugged his shoulders.

"Did you see David yesterday after you got back?"

"I did," Harper said. "He was over with Sarah and the girls for dinner last night."

"How'd he act?"

Harper sat down in the red leather chair in front of Gibson's desk and crossed his legs.

"He was his usual self, even told a couple of jokes. I didn't get a chance to ask him why he had to come in here on Saturday, but he seemed fine. Maybe I'm reading too much into this," the older banker suggested.

"When I came in today I didn't find anything out of order. Maybe it was legit. He's always busy. He was at his desk working by eight," Gibson said.

"David told me he would be here bright and early today, that he had a couple of loan closings to work on."

Harper looked at the calendar on the wall and whined, "Dammit, I forgot about the audit this week. I asked Kevin if he wanted to play golf tomorrow over at Longboat Key. I'd better call him back and cancel. Besides, I have to go down to the islands on Wednesday and get the new account set up. I probably won't be back until the weekend. You can hold down the fort until then, can't you?"

"That won't be a problem Martin. I've got nothing planned this week other than dealing with the feds when they get here."

"Is the accounting firm on board with our paperwork?" the bank president asked.

"Yeah, the accountants came over Friday afternoon and signed off on the documents. That was the last piece of the pie we needed for our little dog and pony show. Other than of course, Thomas' money."

"I have a couple of calls to make, I'll talk to you later," Harper said as he hurried out of Gibson's office.

Harper looked up Kevin Henry's number on his phone and hit the speed dial. It rang a couple of times before a woman answered on the other end.

"Hello, is Kevin there?"

"Hold on one minute please," a female voice on the other end said.

"I don't know who it is," Kevin's girl friend Pamela said as she handed him the phone.

"Kevin, this is Martin. I forgot about the audit this week. Neither Ronnie nor I will be able to play. I have to beg off on our outing tomorrow. I'm sorry about that."

"Don't give it a second thought, Mr. Harper. I have plenty of things I need to do. I just appreciate the offer to play."

"We'll hit the links after we get back from the islands, that's the second reason I called. I want to fly out Wednesday morning. File a flight plan for Grand Cayman Island and St. Thomas. I expect to spend a day on Grand Cayman and possibly three in St. Thomas. I have some business off island so figure our return trip starting on either Saturday or Sunday. I'll book a villa for us on St. John. We can all stay there. Besides, St. John is a lot nicer than St. Thomas."

"I'll file the flight plan tomorrow and make sure we're ready to go early Wednesday morning," the pilot assured him.

"Kevin, you know the fuel capacity of the plane, but I was thinking if we have to stop on the way back, make it in the Caymans."

"I don't think that's going to be necessary. We can fly 6,500 nautical miles. I'll top the tanks off here and we should have a straight shot back."

"Excellent. I'll see you guys at the hangar on Wednesday morning. Let's plan on an eight a.m. departure."

"I'll plan on that and see you then, sir. Goodbye."

Chapter Thirty

ST. MICHAEL'S CHURCH SOCCER FIELD
SIESTA KEY - 7:00 P.M.

"Girls, everybody listen up," Thomas Vasquez implored his soccer team. "This is the only team we haven't beaten this year. I want you to play the trap. Mid fielders play halfway between the center line and the penalty box. I want the fullbacks sitting on the center line. Let's play the game in their end and force them to get the ball out. Everybody put their hands in," Vasquez directed his team.

"One, two, three, let's go!" the coach and girls cheered together.

The eleven girls from St. Michaels walked out on the soccer field wearing their navy blue and white uniforms. The team of seventh and eighth graders lined up and waited for the other team to kick off.

The referee called out to each goalie, checked to see if she was ready and blew his whistle to start the game. The center forward for the other team kicked the ball toward the right fullback of St. Michael. She stopped the ball with her stomach after it bounced in front of her.

She passed the ball forward to the right side of the field, just in front of her mid-fielder. All three lines from St. Michael moved in unison down the field toward the other goal. The right wing caught up to the ball as it rolled in front of her and kicked it past the goalie into the net. The girls and coaches cheered and jumped into the air.

"I love this game," Vasquez yelled out to his assistant coach, Marco.

An hour and a half later the game was over and the girls had defeated their arch-rivals, the Philippi Creek Panthers, by a score of two to one. Vasquez handed out soft drinks to everyone on the team and chatted with the players as everyone walked off the field.

"I'm really proud of what you did today girls. You played a great game, great team effort. Enjoy your drinks, and I'll see you at practice on Friday at six."

All the girls were smiling as they left the field with their parents. The coaches picked up the soccer balls and shoved them into the net bag and followed the players to the parking lot. Vasquez tossed the equipment bag into the trunk of his car.

"Marco, do me a favor. I need you to meet Carlos and Pedro at Selva Grille on Main Street. It's just down from the intersection at Five Points."

"I know where it is boss."

"I'll meet you there in about forty-five minutes. I'm going to stop by the condo and take a quick shower. Here's some cash. Pay for theirs dinners and buy a round of drinks for the three of you. That should cover it."

"Thanks, Mr. V. I'll be happy to take care of this for you."

Vasquez zipped out of the church parking lot and made a right-hand turn on Midnight Pass Road.

He was parking his Mercedes at the Palm Island Club five minutes later. Residents were shuffling to the beach to catch the last glimpse of sunset, something he would have been doing if not for his meeting with Carlos Batista.

After a quick trip up to the tenth floor he entered his apartment a couple of minutes later. His wife was standing by the front balcony window gazing down at the glistening water.

"Elena, the sunset is gorgeous tonight. I wish I could walk the beach with you, but I have to meet with some people. Why don't you go down and enjoy it."

"It's not the same without you, Tomas. Besides, I can sip my Pina Colada from our balcony and take it in. Go ahead and get cleaned up and go to your meeting. I'll be fine. Oh, before I forget, how did the girls do?"

"Elena, the girls played their hearts out and won. I was really happy for them. They're the nicest kids I've ever coached."

"I'm glad they won, dear. I know how hard you work with them and how much you enjoy it."

After a quick shower and a change of clothes he walked back out to the balcony and kissed his wife on the back of the neck.

"I don't know how long our meeting will take, but I'll be back as soon as I can."

"I will wait up for you. Be careful."

He kissed Elena goodbye and bolted for the elevator. A couple of minutes later he was at ground level on his way to his car. After he fastened his seat belt, he looked at the clock on the dashboard—nine o'clock. He was going to be a few minutes late but he could live with that. He bided his time while a stream of sunset gazers moved like ants along the quarter mile driveway.

When he got to Midnight Pass Road he turned left and gunned the engine. Twenty minutes later he was parking the car and crossing Main Street. He saw Robin, the maitre'd, who came over and shook his hand. After a brief conversation he saw his men sitting at a table at the back of the room underneath an art-deco painting illuminated by a soft blue light.

"I trust that Marco has taken care of you in my absence," Vasquez greeted them as he sat down at the table.

"We're doing good boss. Dinner was great, and we had dessert and an after dinner drink," Batista said.

"Good, is everyone ready to go?" Vasquez asked.

"We'll follow you boss," Batista said as the four men got up from the table.

When they left the restaurant Vasquez turned to Marco and said, "I don't think I'm going to need your help anymore tonight. So go and enjoy what is left of the evening."

"Thank you, Mr. V. I think I'll go home, get a shower and kick back."

Batista crossed the street with Vasquez and got into his Mercedes. Estacio backed the green Deville out of a parking space in front of the restaurant and followed the Mercedes. Vasquez turned left on 41 with the Cadillac right behind. When they reached the intersection of Stickney Point and 41, Vasquez made a left on Clark road and drove another five minutes until they reached the self storage location.

"Did you have any problem getting the money stashed in the locker?" Vasquez asked Batista.

"No, but we did have a problem on the way up. Somebody put a bug on one of the trunks."

"Son-of-a-bitch!" Vasquez exploded.

"I only found it because the trunks were moving around in the back. When I got out of the van to secure them, I saw it lying in the back near the door. Tiny little bastard, about the size of an ear plug."

"Where were you when you found it?" Vasquez prodded.

"In a gas station just outside Naples. So I dumped it in another van. When we got up to Ft. Myers, I rented the Caddy and ditched the van in a shopping mall with the keys in the ignition. Somebody will boost it and take the heat if they're picked up. All the cops will find is that it was a stolen rental unit."

"Smart move. Then what did you guys do?" Vasquez asked.

"We came up here, got the storage locker, and dumped the cash."

"You did well, my friend, but the bug bothers me. Do you have any idea how it got there?"

"Not really. I don't think our guy at customs has the stones to be involved. He's too much of a wimp. All I know is that I didn't see it when I picked up the merchandise the day before yesterday. Could have been there, but I didn't see it. And there was nothing funky at our warehouse. The cameras were clean," Batista said.

"Somebody's got us on their shit list. It's time to clean up loose ends. Make the customs man vanish."

"I'll have Sanchez take care of that."

"Make that happen soon," Vasquez demanded.

"I'll call him tonight."

"Speaking of problems, Carlos, have you had any issues lately with the cops in Miami?"

Batista shook his head back and forth and pouted his lips, "No, boss I'm good."

"Carlos, maybe you should stay up here for awhile until things calm down. My gut's telling me Miami is too hot right now."

Chapter Thirty-One

MIAMI BEACH - 9:30 PM

"Look Osborne, you're going to have to stay in this flea bag motel until we figure out what happened," Guzman said as he closed the green metal door behind him.

"It's bad enough you coming to the house and scaring the hell out of my wife, but pulling us out of there doesn't do anybody any good," Osborne griped.

"It works for us and you don't get a vote," Guzman said. "If I thought our operation was compromised, you and your wife would be on a plane to East Jerkwater, New Jersey living a shadow life. But since we still don't know who the bigger fish are, you have no choice. You have to play out the hand that you dealt yourself. That means going to work, going home and then we sneak you out for the night."

"What if they try and snuff me out at work?"

"That's not going to happen. We'll have the place covered. So the game plan for tomorrow is the same as today. Get up and go to work like nothing happened," the agent said.

"What if they call?" Osborne asked with a nervous look.

"Hello! Earth to Osborne! You know they will, they already told you so. Look, we've got a relay to the motel so you won't miss the call. If they ask about the tracking device, play stupid. Act cooperative and don't get flustered. Promise to do whatever they ask. That's how they're going to evaluate your involvement."

"You make everything sound so easy from where you're sitting. It's my ass that's on the line," Osborne pointed out.

Guzman got up from the threadbare brown and red checked dust cover he was sitting on and gave the customs agent a venomous look. "Osborne you're right on the money. But look at it this way. We could have put you in Dade Correctional Institute indefinitely, or we could have just left you out there hanging in the wind. This is as good as it gets."

Guzman narrowed his eyes and pointed a finger at him. "I make only one promise. As long as you are in my custody they aren't going to take you out. I've done this job for awhile, protecting dirt-bags like you in much tougher situations, and I've never lost a witness or informant," Guzman growled.

"You are a real piece of work. You screw up big-time. Then when the going gets tough you want ironclad guarantees. There are no guarantees when you're dealing with bad ass drug dealers."

Then he fired one last salvo, "You should have thought about that before you took the first payoff."

Chapter Thirty-Two

GULFCOAST BANK, SARASOTA - 9:45 PM

Thomas Vasquez handed Gibson a computer printout. "We have four containers, a little over ten-million dollars. Here's the breakdown of the load that they gave me. My people counted it on the other end. So it's your choice Ronnie, whether to count it now or later."

"Thomas, your guys are always right on the mark; and since it's so late I'll do it tomorrow. I'll make the entry for your company tomorrow and you'll be squared away. Martin and I talked earlier, we'll move the money next week just before the next shipment comes in."

Vasquez paused. "Is everything all right here at the bank?"

Gibson was caught off-guard by the question as he watched the men bring the last chest into the vault and unload the stacks of hundred dollar bills.

"What do you mean, Thomas?" Gibson said as his brow tightened.

"Are there any problems with any of the employees at the bank? Has anyone been snooping around trying to get information on me? What about the government?"

"We have a routine audit that begins tomorrow and it should be over the following day. As far as anybody asking about you, the only person within the bank was David Dreyer."

"What do you mean?" Vasquez said as he gave a wary look.

"He was asking Martin about your company and the syndicated underwriting of your new condominium complex. Since he's the chief loan officer of the bank, it wasn't an off-the-wall question," Gibson said.

"He is suspicious of us. Why would he ask if he didn't think there was a problem?"

Gibson walked away from the vault door. "Thomas, guys in David's position look at every transaction with some degree of skepticism. That's the nature of the beast. Credit scores, rates of return, and exposure levels are what they live and breathe. I do business on a handshake. He doesn't. You know we have loan committee meetings to document all this crap for the government. My deals are approved before we ever meet. He goes strictly by the book."

Vasquez brow furrowed. "Was he against the bank doing the project?"

"No, he was on board for the condominium deal, but Martin's running it, not him. That's why I think he asked the question to begin with. Martin talked to him and he seemed satisfied. He's a micro-manager."

"So you are certain that he's not a problem," the Columbian persisted.

"I don't think so. He came into work Saturday when we were in Washington, but Martin didn't think it was a big deal. Then he saw him last night for dinner and said everything was fine."

"Really? Keep an eye on him just the same."

"You worry too much, Thomas!"

"And you don't worry enough, my friend," Vasquez said as he shot back a look that could kill.

"Thomas, we have to get out of here. The cleaning crew is due shortly."

"Yeah, I have to get going too. I'm sure my friends are getting antsy waiting outside for me. I'll talk to you later in the week about the next shipment." Vasquez ambled toward the exit at the rear of the bank.

When he got into his car he turned to Batista and asked, "Would it be easier to do a tap on the phones or place a bug inside an office?"

"Depends on the location and what the business is."

"What about the bank?" Vasquez asked.

He put the car in gear and drove out of the bank parking lot, waiting for the answer.

"That's easy, a bug. Too many problems trying to do a phone tap. If their security is any good they would pick it up. The bank has an outside cleaning crew don't they?"

"Yeah, they have a crew, why?"

"Because that's the easiest way I found to put bugs and wiretaps inside a building. Nobody gives the cleaning crew a second look. Plus, they have free run of the building once they get inside."

"Have you ever had any problems with these guys becoming an issue once they worked for you?" Vasquez asked.

"No, you give a cleaning crew guy five bills to plant a bug and promise him another five if the information is good and that usually keeps them in line. A grand for five minutes of work is a month's salary to these guys. Never saw one who wouldn't jump at the chance. In fact, once they do it they want to go in business with you at other places they work," Batista explained.

Vasquez laughed for the first time since he had picked his men up. He drove into the South entrance of Gulf Gate shopping mall and Estacio followed him into the parking lot. He pulled into an empty parking space near the back of the Pizzaro Bread Store. Batista waited for his partner to pull alongside.

"Carlos, you never cease to amaze me," Vasquez said. "You know how to get to people and manipulate them. That's a gift, an underappreciated asset in business."

"I just do what needs to be done."

"So do I. That's why we've been together so long. If you ever need anything, don't hesitate to ask. It's yours."

"I'll keep that in mind, boss."

"Here's a token of my appreciation for the job you did in Washington," Vasquez said as he handed him an envelope. Then he reached into his pocket, pulled out a roll of hundred dollar bills and handed half of them to Carlos. "You guys hang out at the Hyatt for awhile. I'll be in touch."

"*Gracias*, boss."

"No, I owe you, Carlos. It is me who should be thanking you. Enjoy your night," Vasquez told him as he climbed out of the Mercedes.

Batista counted the money with his back to Estacio. It was his largest payday ever, twenty thousand dollars. He put the envelope inside his pocket, climbed into the passenger seat, turned to Estacio and said, "Go north on 41 to the Hyatt. We'll get a couple of rooms, go up town and check out the Sarasota nightlife."

Chapter Thirty-Three

D.O.J.-WASHINGTON D.C., TUESDAY - 8:00 AM

"Who wants to begin?" Brune asked his investigators.

"I will," Trupp volunteered. He opened his briefcase and pulled out a yellow legal pad and laid it on the walnut colored desk.

"We think Batista stayed at the Best Western in Roslyn. The lady at the front desk recognized his photo. He used some alias. His room had been cleaned, but we got a couple of partial prints and are checking them out. Unfortunately, we're a day late and a dollar short there, and at a dead end on the forensic evidence from the car."

"Did you get any useful information from Harrington's wife?"

"Nah, we drew a blank," Trupp said. Nothing at the Harrington's house in Silver Springs or at their primary residence in Charleston. His wife was unaware of any threatening phone calls or mail. She was pretty much out of the loop where he was concerned. In fact, she said he only came home to Charleston a couple of weekends each month when

Congress was in session. That's where she lived most of the time. Said he was a busy man."

"You got that right. Busy jumping every woman he could in D.C.," Brune said as he tapped his fingers on the desk. "Rich, what do you have?"

"I think I may have found a possible link. One that ties his contributions to legislation he sponsored."

"Really?" the top agent said as he sat up and leaned on the desk.

"It involves banking regulations and laws to protect his biggest contributors from them. I had to go back and check regulatory law to see how the legislation impacted it and vice versa. Harrington was second on the Banking Committee and head of Ways and Means. So he was in charge of marking up every single bill for consideration. He and Murphy were a two-man steamroller. He, or someone on his committee would mark up the finance bills. Murphy's committee would pass them and bring them to the Senate floor for the vote. But it was Harrington who ushered them all the way through the process," Herzog explained.

"Rich, this confirms our read of Murphy. Go on."

"Money flowed out of the 527 committees Harrington controlled to various senators. They got money and access to him, which meant favorable treatment on their pet legislation. In return they either sponsored or supported his bills. Based on what I saw regarding legislation that he marked up, it was a classic quid pro quo."

Herzog took a sip of coffee and continued. "He carved his niche in banking. If you wanted his help you had to pay for his influence. Like I said the other day, it's a laundry list of corporate banking in America. More banking legislation was passed during the past four sessions than was passed in the prior twelve."

"This town is such a cesspool of money and power," Trupp said.

Brune nodded. "Campaign finance reform is an oxymoron. A campaign contribution is nothing more than a bribe, and incumbents are money whores. They will never stop the flow of cash," Brune scoffed.

Herzog picked up his notes. "Getting back to the report, Harper was the ringleader for the 527 committees for both Harrington and Murphy. Gulfcoast Bank and Caribbean Ventures were the two largest corporate contributors. Harper and a guy by the name of Thomas Vasquez are connected to both companies. These are the ones we have to look at the hardest."

"You need to go down to Sarasota and check these guys out," Brune said. "I can pull their background checks with federal and state and see what pops up, but we need much more than that. We need biographical data on them, their companies, their employees, their customer base, their personal lives, everything."

"Won't we need court orders to do that?" Trupp asked.

"We will Russ, but I won't have a problem getting you guys blanket subpoenas and wiretaps after I show a judge what we have. That's the most efficient way to proceed. Turn over every rock where these guys are concerned," Brune instructed.

"Now that we know where to look, maybe some of this will begin to make sense," Trupp offered.

"While you guys are proceeding on that front I'm going to go after Carlos Batista," Brune declared. "He looks like the guy who will open the floodgates for us. He's ex-military from Columbia. The FBI forwarded me his INS file. He came into the country from Cartagena the same time as another ex-military man, Thomas Vasquez."

"No shit," Trupp said as he pulled his chair closer to Brune's desk.

"It gets better. DEA in Miami has another Columbian, Pedro Estacio, on their radar screen. I talked with Agent Guzman in the Miami DEA office. Estacio and another Columbian are involved in a bribery scheme with a customs agent. I've already sent him a copy of Batista's picture to see if he's the other guy involved in their investigation. Guzman's supposed to get back to me later today. He doesn't know what they're moving, but it's either drugs or money. Told me it's a big operation, every couple of weeks. When you get down to Florida I want you to meet with him. See if we can connect all the dots. See what role Vasquez has in all this."

"When do you want us to go down there?" Herzog asked.

"As soon as possible."

"I probably need another day to wrap up what I have," Herzog said. "What about you, Russ?"

"Thursday works for me. Do you need any of my guys to help you check out people here in DC?"

"As a matter of fact I do. Harrington's assistant gave the names of a half-dozen women."

Herzog fished inside his small leather brief case and laid it in front of Trupp. "Here's the list. Can your guys run them down?"

"Yeah, not a problem," the detective told him as he looked down at the names on the sheet.

"My impression from her was that these women were flings, nothing more, but we have to clear them to move forward," Herzog told him.

"Yeah, my guys will check them out."

"I'm in a little bit of a time crunch. I appreciate the help. I have to go over and talk to Murphy and Harrington's admin."

"Sounds like you two have your work cut out for you. While you guys are doing that, I'll start dissecting Harper's and Vasquez' corporate tax returns. Let's plan on meeting again tomorrow morning," Brune said.

"Oh, before I forget it Rich, here's a DOJ internal memo." Brune handed him a document and said, "You might find it useful if the good senator has a memory lapse or needs a little encouragement."

"Timing's everything. This was a piece of legislation that caught my eye yesterday," Herzog said as he tucked the paper in his brief case."

"Your instincts were right on the mark. Good luck with the Murphy."

Chapter Thirty-Four

SENATOR MURPHY'S OFFICE - 10:00 AM

"Thanks for taking the time to meet with me again Senator," Herzog said as he shook his hand and entered his private office. The agent sat down across the desk from Murphy.

"Like I told you before, any way I can help I will. Do you care for some coffee or a pastry? We have a gourmet bakery on the mezzanine level," the senator offered.

"Thanks, I've already had something this morning," Herzog answered.

"These are killer pecan rolls," Murphy said as he took a bite.

"Is that from a taste or cholesterol perspective?" Herzog asked with a grin.

"Unfortunately, both. Now, what can I do for you?" the legislator asked.

"Senator, I've been looking back at the contribution list for Senator Harrington and the legislation that he either marked up or referred to your committee. I would like to know what your involvement has been with Martin Harper and Thomas Vasquez?"

Murphy put his coffee down so quick he almost tipped it over. He wiped his lips with a napkin, sat back in his chair and took a deep breath before responding. Herzog had hit a nerve, as he knew he would. He wasn't about to be subtle with the senator. He wanted Murphy to confirm much of what he already knew and fill in the missing blanks for him.

"I was introduced to these two gentlemen by John Harrington. We met at a fund-raiser at the Sawgrass Golf Course in Florida a number of years back. They've been, shall we say, substantial contributors to both of our campaigns since."

"I was aware of that from the financial records," Herzog interjected.

Murphy proceeded, "Because of their value to us we generally get together with them a couple of times a year at fund-raisers and charity golf events. Here and in Florida. What else do you want to know?" he said indignantly.

"There's been a significant amount of legislation passed through your committee in the last two sessions. In doing a cursory read it looks like the banking industry has been shielded from a lot of regulatory action. In other words, bills came out of your committee for the full Senate to vote on that protected the banks. And every one passed," Herzog said.

Murphy smiled nervously and said, "Look, our constituents make us aware of their needs, what their problems are, and when we can, we help them. That's the way this town has always operated. The simple fact is if we don't make an effort to take care of constituents, they have the resources to find an opponent who will."

Herzog leaned forward in his chair. "Senator, that's where I'm having trouble. I get the picture on the job security issue. But Harrington's committee marked up a bill that if passed would have limited disclosure information on sources of money coming into the country. The exemption law for multinational corporations on the transfer of large sums of money out of the country was another piece that was marked up and didn't pass. Those are the two I want to know about."

Murphy tossed his Danish into a trash can in the corner. "Dammit! I knew those two pieces of legislation would come back to haunt me."

"Tell me about them," Herzog prodded.

"A week before Bubba got killed he came to me about resurrecting those two bills. They both failed by a couple of votes on the floor the week before and he wanted me to have them marked up again through my committee. There wasn't enough time left in this session to run them through my committee and get them to the floor for a vote. So when he came to me I told him I couldn't do it before summer recess. Harrington told me that I had to, that his constituents needed them passed. Hell, I never had the time to read either of the bills. Someone on my staff did the research."

"Really," Herzog said.

"There was no way I could run it through my committee, which meant neither piece had any way of getting to the floor for a vote. And he couldn't get it put on as a rider to existing legislation that was pending. The rules prohibit adding them once House and Senate conferees have omnibus legislation under review. You can put in earmarks for money to go back to your district right up unit the last minute, but not substantive legislation," the senator stipulated.

"Did he tell you who needed this?"

"No. He didn't volunteer and I didn't want to know. For the very reason you and I are having this conversation right now. I'm not a lawyer, but it never passed the smell test on the first go-round. I wasn't about to put my name on it a second time," Murphy growled.

"What was his reaction?"

"He was pissed! It was as if he was counting on me to bail his ass out and I failed him. In fact, he told me that I owed it to him after everything he had done for me over the years."

"In other words Senator Harrington was calling in your marker?" Herzog asked in a mock tone of voice.

"Yeah, I guess that's how he viewed it. I sure as hell didn't. As far as I was concerned he needed me more than I needed him. I only introduced a couple of proposals every session. Everything else that came out of my committee was by other members, the majority of them at his behest."

A disgusted look registered on Murphy's face.

"So where did you leave it when the meeting ended?" Herzog said.

"He told me he would do what he had to and stormed out of the office. That was the last time we spoke." Murphy stared away for a couple of seconds.

"Senator," Herzog said trying to get his attention back.

"Sorry," Murphy said as he focused back on the agent. "Now what were you saying?"

"I want you to read this DOJ memo on counter-terrorism and funding. Look to the footnotes at the bottom and see what two pieces of legislation are highlighted."

Herzog slid the papers over to the senator. Murphy threw the report back down on his desk after reading it. "Son of a bitch!"

"Senator, you did the right thing. Your instincts were correct," the agent said as he reached over and took the report back.

"Not on the first go around," he muttered.

Then the senator leaned forward and asked, "Does this mean that I'm the subject of a Justice Department investigation?"

"Not that I know of."

"Let me take it one step further. Do you think the legislation and his murder are connected, given the content of the memo?" Murphy asked in a panicked voice.

The investigator considered it and said, "The truth is, I really don't know at this time because I don't know who was pushing his buttons. Somebody wanted the legislation back on track for a reason. Have you had any contact with anyone since his death, about these two legislative proposals?"

"No, I haven't. Do you think somebody will contact me? Could I be a target?" the legislator said as he loosened the knot on his tie

"Interesting point, given what you've told me," Herzog fired back. "Let's err on the side of caution. I want to tap your phones, both here and at your home. I also want you to have a bodyguard around the clock. I can have someone here in twenty minutes, unless of course, you would rather have one of your own security people."

"I can get Lieutenant Swisshelm from Capitol Police. He's worked with my office in the past. He's a decorated Gulf War veteran, a good man," the senator said.

"I also need you to sign a letter of authorization for the wiretap on your stationery with your administrative assistant signing as a witness. You can trust her can't you?" Herzog pressed.

"With my life."

The agent shoved a piece of paper across the desk. "Good, we'll get that end started and I'll have somebody over here in a little while putting the taps on the phones."

Chapter Thirty-Five

SENATOR HARRINGTON'S OFFICE - 12:00 PM

"Adrienne, I apologize about the time. My meeting took longer than I expected," Herzog explained as he entered her office.

"Don't give it a second thought, Richard. I have plenty to do getting ready for the senator's replacement. Come in, sit down," she told him.

The agent relaxed in an oversized tufted leather chair.

"I read in the Times that Mrs. Poudre was appointed by the governor to fill out his term. Didn't she serve in the House for a couple of terms?" he asked.

"Yes, she did. That was after a lucrative, fifteen year career on Wall Street as an investment banker. She's an incredibly smart woman. It will be great to work with her. Mrs. Poudre called and wants to keep the staff intact. She plans on being here tomorrow and getting started."

"Sounds like she's coming on board with an atypical beltway mentality," the agent said.

"You're absolutely correct. Mrs. Poudre has intelligence and she has integrity. She took this job as a favor to the governor, not as a career move. That is as altruistic as it gets. She's doing this as a public service. I couldn't be more pleased that she's the replacement," Adrienne asserted.

She paused. "I tend to get off on these tangents Richard, I'm sorry. By the way I loved our little get together at lunch the other day. I'd like to see you again, away from the office after all this mess gets straightened out. I know you're busy and don't have the time right now. But I want you to think about it. I like being with you."

Her lips parted and her skin became flushed, dying to hear his answer

"You never cease to amaze me, Adrienne. I can't tell you how much I enjoyed the other day."

She smiled from ear to ear, hanging on every word.

"I'd like to do that. But as you said, I'm really busy now. But I promise we will see each other again."

"I had to tell you how I felt Richard. I've been thinking about you a lot since then," she continued.

"I'm glad you did, because I've been doing the same thing, Adrienne."

Herzog smiled, relieved because he was able to bring himself to break the ice and tell her how he felt.

"So how can I help you today?"

"In the days leading up to Senator Harrington's death did he confide in you about any concerns that he might have had? Did he say or do anything that would lead you to believe he felt threatened?"

Adrienne thought about it and said, "He was in the office on Monday of the week he died. The senator signed some papers and we talked a little about his schedule and what was coming up. He seemed agitated and spent most of the day on the phone. He was definitely anxious about something. He never told me what was bothering him. I didn't see him at all Tuesday or Wednesday, but he called in both days."

"Hmmm. Do you know where he called from?" Herzog asked.

"He could have been back in Charleston, but I think he was still in town because he told me he was going to the Israeli Embassy party that week."

"Have you or your legislative assistant had any inquiries regarding legislation since the shooting? Or for that matter, has anyone approached you to set up a meeting with Mrs. Poudre?"

Adrienne looked down at some papers on her desk. "No one in the office has received any requests regarding legislation since the senator's death. As for meetings, we've had requests for a number of them. I have the list right here."

She handed him the list.

"But as I recall, the majority are with other people here on the Hill and a couple of media requests. There may be a constituent or two sprinkled throughout. But I think they were just meet-and-greet deals."

Herzog handed the list back to her. "Thanks, Adrienne. When you were clearing out his desk, did you come across any information written down on scratch paper or legal pads?"

"No, I gave you everything I found from his desk and his office the other day," she confirmed.

"All right, I'll go over the phone logs again and see who the senator talked to in the days leading up to the shooting. Maybe something will turn up," Herzog added.

Almost as an afterthought Herzog said, "Did the names of Martin Harper or Thomas Vasquez come up in conversation that last week?"

"No, he didn't speak to me about either Mr. Harper or Mr. Vasquez."

"Adrienne, if either of these men contact your office call me immediately."

"Of course I will." She followed that with a strange look, but didn't say anything.

"I'll be in touch," Herzog assured her.

"Promise?"

Chapter Thirty-Six

SARASOTA AIRPORT, WEDNESDAY - 9:00 AM

"Is the boss settled in back there?" Kevin Henry asked his co-pilot.

"He is. We're good to go. I secured the door, he's reading his paper and drinking a cup of coffee."

"Let Mr. Harper know we've finished the pre-flight check. We have clearance for takeoff on runway two west," the chief pilot told Paul.

The co-pilot picked up the intercom phone. "Good morning, Mr. Harper. We've been cleared by the tower and will be airborne shortly. We're second in line, we'll be heading out over the Gulf in a couple of minutes and follow the coastline down to Miami. After we clear the Miami corridor, we'll head west over the Gulf of Mexico and on down to Grand Cayman. Our ETA should be around 11:00 AM. The forecast is for mostly clear skies with some patchy clouds so it should be smooth sailing all the way down."

"Thanks for the update, Paul. I'm strapped in and ready to go."

Kevin eased the yoke back and the Gulfstream began to pick up speed. A minute later they were soaring above the outer marker at a hundred and fifty knots. When they reached three thousand feet and were two miles out over the Gulf, the jet banked 30 degrees to the south and continued to climb. Kevin looked down at the sun-drenched Sarasota shoreline as it glistened out the left side of the aircraft.

Paul was busy checking the instruments and looking at the navigational charts on his computer screen as he always did during the first part of the flight. When they had reached their cruising altitude of twenty-five thousand feet, Kevin turned over the flight controls to Paul. He took his head set off, stood up and headed through the cockpit door. On his way back to the galley he thought about how much he loved to fly, especially this custom fitted jewel of an aircraft.

Despite the fact that the Gulfstream had an autopilot that was computer controlled neither pilot used it very much. They liked flying the aircraft. It was every pilot's dream to be able to be at the controls from either seat on a plane like this.

The aircraft was literally a state of the art piece of machinery. A flight cabin with the most advanced avionics in the industry and BMW-Rolls Royce engines that slung the plane through the air like a slingshot at over 460 knots cruising speed. Teakwood panels adorned the walls. A flat screen TV was on the bulkhead wall. Tufted, reclining captains chairs, each with individual head sets, and a leather sofa that folded out into a small bed made the interior look more like a suite at a posh hotel than the cabin of an airplane. These were but a part of the reasons that pilots and passengers sought out the plane.

As he passed by Harper reading his copy of Investors Business Daily, the pilot stopped and asked him if he wanted another cup of coffee.

"No thanks, Kevin. One's plenty for me."

The pilot searched the galley looking for a couple of plastic cups because he didn't want to use the good china for their coffees. He found a roll of them tucked inside one of the cabinets. He poured two cups of coffee and went back to the cockpit. Kevin handed one to his co-pilot and sat down with the other. He made a quick check of the flight instruments and took another sip of coffee. A few minutes later he checked in with Miami Flight Center who transmitted his new coordinates.

They confirmed his location on their radar screen and gave him permission to follow his flight plan which took them around the northwest coast of Cuba. Kevin had a brief exchange about territorial airspace and maintaining control with the flight center at Miami and signed off.

"Miami Control wants us to take a more westerly route. The new heading is three-three-zero. I'll put the information in the computer while you change our flight path."

The plane took a gradual turn to the west and straightened out. Within minutes they were approaching the northwest tip of Cuba. Once they were safely outside Cuban airspace they banked to the south and headed toward Grand Cayman Island. Ten minutes later Kevin called back to the rear of the plane.

"Mr. Harper, we just received permission from Grand Cayman Tower to land. We'll start our descent shortly and be landing in about fifteen minutes."

"Thanks, Kevin. I'll get back in my seat and buckle up shortly."

As the Gulfstream made its final approach above the translucent blue waters of the Caribbean, Kevin was again reminded why he loved flying so much. It wasn't work. It was seeing the world with a bird's eye view from the heavens above. Another day, another island, another country, it didn't matter. It wasn't just part of his life. It was what he lived for, and he didn't want the merry-go-round to stop. That was another reason the thought of going to the government about the contraband cargo bothered him so much. It was going to cost him as well.

Fifteen minutes later Paul made a feather-soft landing on the sun baked concrete strip and taxied the plane to the far end of the terminal— the area reserved for general aviation aircraft and small commuter planes. Kevin went back to the exit door and unlocked it. He pushed the button, and the steps unfolded down to the tarmac. A blast of hot air shot through the doorway.

"I love coming to the islands," Harper said as he retrieved his briefcase and sunglasses from the bench seat across the aisle.

"Yes sir, it's pretty intoxicating," Kevin said as the jet turbo fans whistled to a stop.

As he prepared to walk down the steps he turned to his pilot and said, "Why don't you guys go over to Seven Mile Beach and hang out there for awhile? I don't know how long my deal is going to take today. Keep your cell phones on. I'll call you and let you know if we are staying here or going on to St. Thomas."

"Will do, Mr. Harper," Kevin said.

The banker hustled across the tarmac and into the terminal. He showed his diplomatic papers to an immigration official and shot past a line of incoming passengers. A chauffeur met him at the door and escorted him to a dark green Mercedes.

"Benturro, good to see you again. I want to go to the Banco Nationale," the banker told him.

"Yes sir, Mr. Harper. Sit back and enjoy the ride. There are bottles of mineral water, soda, wine and beer in the bar if you want something cool. Or liquor and some ice if you care for a mixed drink."

"Thanks. I'm a bit parched," Harper told him as he reached to open the bar.

He pulled out a cold bottle of mineral water took a quick drink and gazed out at the topaz blue water and the condominiums that stretched for miles. The little island that he first visited twenty years ago was booming. Condominiums were sprouting up like mushrooms and traffic was heavy. With over 500 financial institutions doing business on the main island, Grand Cayman had the greatest concentration of banking per square mile in the world.

Twenty minutes later the chauffeur pulled the car into the parking lot under the shade of a thirty-foot Cuban palm. He opened the door and Harper grabbed his briefcase and bottle of water and walked into the bank.

The manager greeted him as soon as he stepped into the entryway.

"Mr. Harper, it is a pleasure to see you again."

"Thank you Geoffrey, it's nice to be back," Harper said as the two men shook hands. "I was sorry to read about your friend Senator Harrington. Nasty business, the shooting and all," the manager said in a consoling tone.

"Yes it was, and the authorities still don't seem to have much of a handle on the case."

"Why don't we go back into the boardroom where we can have a little more privacy?"

Harper followed Parsons to the rear of the bank into a large meeting room. Peach colored plaster walls and a solid mahogany door guaranteed the anonymity of anyone conducting business there. A mahogany table, sixteen feet long and four feet wide, took up the center of the room. A bar, refrigerator and food preparation area were located in a separate room to the right of the table.

"Before we get started would you like some other refreshment, or perhaps something to eat?" the banker offered.

"Thank you Geoffrey, but I'm good with my water."

"When you spoke to me last week you told me that you wanted to open another account that you could tie in with your existing account. I can do that, but we will have to establish a subsidiary corporation first. Once that's completed we have to show a banking relationship with the parent company by transferring funds out of your existing corporate account into the new one," the manager told Harper.

"That's perfect. I was hoping we could do that, but I wasn't sure what the banking laws stipulated here," Harper said.

"Essentially, what we have here is a means for the parent company to both deposit and withdraw from the subsidiary company. The subsidiary company will have no access to the parent company funds. That is what you want to do, correct?"

"That's it in a nutshell Geoffrey."

"Very good then. I have drawn up the papers of incorporation. I will need you to sign the documents. You can have as many as three parties who have signing authority on the account. I will give you the paperwork for the other signatures and you can mail that back to me at your discretion. What I need today is your signature on the paperwork to get the account online."

· Parsons pushed a folder across the table. "This last set of papers for you to sign is our equivalent of your Homeland Security financial laws. Just not as transparent," the manager assured him.

"I assume you want me to date all the paperwork today?" Harper said.

"That would be correct."

"I was thinking of an initial transfer of one million in U.S. currency from the existing account. How soon will the subsidiary company be up and running?" Harper wanted to know.

"I may be able to get it filed by today, but tomorrow for sure," Parsons promised.

"You're the best Geoffrey. Back home this would take weeks to do. Let's call the name of the new company Gulf and Bay Enterprises."

"Very well then, that's what the title will read," Parsons said as he jotted the information down on a legal pad.

"I'll call you on Thursday or Friday with the account number of the other subsidiary I'm setting up in Tortola. It's going to be the same company, different location, and of course we'll have to conform to their laws. You said they were very similar to yours," Harper asked.

"That's correct. You shouldn't have any problems. A five-hundred dollar corporate filing fee is the only real difference. It will be up and running the same day or next, just like here. My colleague in Road Town is Lionel Smith. I can call him if you like and he will have everything ready when you walk into the office," Parsons volunteered.

"That would save me precious time if you could do that."

"Consider it done."

"This didn't take as long as I thought it would take," the Florida banker brimmed.

"I am always happy to assist you in any way I can Mr. Harper. You have been a valued customer. The bank appreciates all of your business and the many customers you have referred to us over the years."

"Geoffrey, thanks for all your help," Harper told him as he stood to shake hands. "You should be seeing electronic money transfers into the new company within the next couple of days."

"Very good, sir. Have a safe trip down island," Parsons told him as he led him to the door.

"Thanks again for everything Geoffrey, and have a good day."

As soon as he got back into the car Harper dialed his pilot's cell phone.

"Kevin, I was able to complete my business transaction a lot sooner than I anticipated. If we could, I'd like to fly down to St. Thomas this afternoon."

"Sure, we can do that. I filed the flight plan with the control center at the airport before we headed over to the beach. All we have to do is get on the plane, get clearance from the tower and go."

"Yes," Harper said, elated that they could fly down to the Virgin Islands the same day. "I'll see you guys on the tarmac."

Chapter Thirty-Seven

GULFCOAST BANK, SARASOTA - 7:00 PM

The cleaning crew arrived just as Ronnie Gibson was leaving his office. He had survived the first day of the audit and was glad to be leaving work. He opened the door to his Porsche 911, pulled a joint from the crude foil pack under his floor mat and lit it up. He held the smoke in for a couple of seconds before exhaling. One more day to go and the feds would be history he told himself as he took another hit. Then he turned the ignition key, put the Porsche in gear and shot out of the lot.

The four man crew from Siesta Key Cleaning Company had entered the bank a little after seven o'clock. Eduardo Morales, the crew chief, was busy going through the offices dumping papers from the waste containers near each desk. The rest of the crew was busy vacuuming the carpets, dusting off the tables and counter tops, and sweeping the marble floors in the entry area.

After tossing a half dozen plastic trash bags into the dumpster behind the bank Morales came back inside. He went over to a woman sweeping the marble floor and told her to begin mopping the surface when she finished. Then he met with two other members of the crew and told them to begin cleaning the glass doors and interior windows.

Having made sure that everyone was occupied, Morales strolled back into the office of David Dreyer. He closed the door behind him and fumbled in his jacket pocket a couple of seconds before he found the tiny transmitter. It was about the size of a small button.

The janitor looked around the room trying to decide where to place the listening device. He stuck it under the desk drawer, got up, and dialed his cell phone.

"I got the bug in place. What do you want me to do?"

"Hang up your cell phone. Then walk around the room and talk to me in a normal tone of voice," Batista told him.

The janitor switched the phone off and marched around the room repeating, "Can you hear me? Can you hear me?"

A half a minute later his cell phone rang and he pressed the dial.

"We're good. Come outside and I'll give you the rest of your money," Batista said.

When Morales walked past the lady mopping the floor, she looked up at him.

"I forgot my cell phone, and I didn't want to use a land line since I just cleaned all of them," he explained.

He locked the door behind him and ambled over to the dark green Cadillac parked on the other side of his truck. The tinted window cracked open a couple of inches, and he was handed a plain white envelope with a rubber band wrapped around it.

"We'll talk later," the driver said as the window closed.

The car sped away. The crew chief slowly counted the hundred dollar bills inside. He stuffed it into the inside pocket of his jacket and walked back inside the bank.

Chapter Thirty-Eight

SARASOTA, FLORIDA – 8:30 PM

"So how did the audit go today?" Sarah Dreyer asked.

"OK I guess, but I really don't know. I was gone for the majority of the day. Even if I had been there I would have been clueless. With a typical audit they keep asking for data, and it's usually up to the bank manager to answer their every beck and call. I'm sure that's what Ronnie was doing all day long."

"Is dinner OK?" Sarah asked.

"Yeah, the tilapia is just great. Did the girls like it?" David Dreyer said as he took a drink of his Sauvignon Blanc.

"What little they had to eat. They took a couple of bites and headed over to school for the soccer game. Are you all right, David? I know you're preoccupied with the bank, but I have never seen you like this," Sarah said.

He put his fork down and peered across the table. Her shoulders were hunched down, and she sat with her hands in her lap. "When we talked about the situation at the bank the other day I couldn't tell you a lot because I didn't know everything that was

going on," he said. "Now I do, and it's really ugly.
You're going to have to trust me on this when I tell
you, that the less you know the better off we'll be."

"What are you talking about, David?" his wife
said through the lump in her throat

Dreyer reached over and laid a tiny white
envelope down on the white linen place mat sitting in
front of her. "Here is the key to a safe deposit box
over at the Provident Bank branch on Beneva. I want
you to hide the key and not tell anyone about it. It
contains documents and a disc with information about
the bank. This is just an insurance policy. I'm going to
talk to the FBI after the audit is finished."

Sarah struggled to ask, "Is daddy involved?"

"I don't see how he couldn't be."

Sarah lifted her napkin to her cheek and
dabbed at her eyes. Dreyer got up, went over and sat
down next to her. He put his arm around her shoulder
as she began to well up.

"Sarah, I love you. We'll get through this. I
promise."

Chapter Thirty-Nine

CINCINNATI, OHIO - 9:00 PM

The door chime rang. Corky Millner turned away from the Cincinnati Reds baseball game on his 50 inch plasma television and knocked over his bottle of Michelob. "Dammit," he said as he picked up the overturned bottle and ran to the kitchen for a towel.

"Hang on, I'll be there in a second," he yelled as he blotted the carpet.

He glanced at his watch and muttered, "The pizza delivery guy got here a lot faster than I thought he would."

Millner hustled to the door and swung it open "Corky Millner?"

"Yeah, that's me."

"DEA. We have a warrant to search the premises," a tall black man dressed in a leather bomber jacket and jeans told him as he flashed his badge and showed him the papers.

"Are you shitting me?" Millner said as he backed away.

Two other agents dressed in camouflage fatigues walked past him toward the back of his condominium. Millner slammed the door, shuffled into the living room and fell back into his tan colored sofa.

"My name is Gibbs. We need to talk," the agent announced. He sat down next to him in a rust colored wing back chair.

"Are we going to find any of your stash here?"

"What stash?" Millner said in a brash tone.

"You might as well tell me because we have you on at least one charge of selling five grams of cocaine to one of my guys. But today could be your lucky day if you cooperate. Turns out I want your supplier more than I want you."

Time stood still for a few seconds while Millner tried to process what was going down. He ran his hand across his forehead, turned to the agent and asked. "So what are you offering?"

A voice from the bedroom interrupted the agent before he could answer. "Ask him where he's got the coke stashed. I'm getting tired of looking."

"What I'm offering is a chance for you to walk away from this. No arrest, no arraignment, no jail time. It would be like none of this ever happened."

Millner's eye brows lifted, "And in return?"

"You tell me who your supplier is."

"I tell you who my supplier is and I'm a dead man," Millner growled. "That isn't even a debate. You couldn't begin to hide me from this guy. Hell, I could do a few years in the joint standing on my head. At least I'd be alive," the drug dealer said as he flashed him a wary look.

"Speaking of jail time, how do you feel about your girlfriend getting charged as an accessory to your little operation? We can show that you made phone calls from her condo and that makes her an accomplice. Who knows what a search warrant would dredge up at her place?"

"You suck! I can't believe you would bring her into this," the dealer shouted.

"I'm not bringing her into this, you are— or not, depending on whether you cooperate."

Millner stood up and began to pace back and forth mumbling to himself. "Heh, I need some time to think this over."

Gibbs looked at his watch, "Fine, no problem, you've got two minutes."

The other agents came back into the living room shaking their heads.

"Run his phone records for the land line and the cell. I want to know everybody he's talked to for the past couple of years."

"Will do, sir," one of the agents said as they walked into the kitchen.

The agent tapped his wrist watch. "So what's it going to be?"

"Look, this guy has a long reach. Even if you bust him, and he serves the rest of his life in jail he can still get to me. He's bad news. If I had known how evil this guy was I would never have gone into business with him in the first place. Talk about having a pact with the devil. This guy is it," Millner vouched.

"I'll give you a little something else to think about. Federal sentencing guidelines have been revamped. You're going to do more than three to five because of your prior conviction. You know the piggyback effect?"

The DEA agent paused then gave him the ultimatum, "So you're going to take the deal?"

Millner nodded. "Tell me exactly what you're prepared to do for me. Witness relocation, a new life, what?"

"All of the above if this is the guy we think he is," the agent promised.

"All right, we got a deal, but I'm going to need it in writing," he muttered.

"So who is Mr. Big?"

Millner stared at the agent and said, "I only met him once and that was when I was down in south Florida. I don't have a clue what his name is. My friend Luis told me he was from Colombia. Said this guy used to be in the Army down there. I assumed he lived in Miami."

"So how many people you got dealing for you?"

"Just a couple of guys."

"We're going to need their names, addresses and cell phone numbers," the agent told him as he tossed his notepad on the coffee table in front of Millner.

"Where do you pick up your supply?"

"Louisville, Knoxville, St. Louis. Sometimes they bring it here. I never know. It's always a different location."

"So let's get back to this Colombian. How did you meet this guy?"

"My friend Luis, who was a dealer down there, set it up. This Colombian is the scariest bastard I ever crossed paths with in my life. My one and only meeting took place in some ramshackle motel near the Miami River. We're talking our shit haggling about price with a couple of bangers, and this guy who looks like Juan Valdez busts into the room sporting a Mac 10. I got ten grand sitting in a suitcase on the bed. I grab the suitcase and bolt for the window on the second floor, ready to do a swan dive down to the concrete two floors below. He unloads a magazine clip into the ceiling and that stopped me in my tracks. I figure I'd better listen to what he has to say."

"Then what?"

"He motioned me to sit down on the bed. I did. Then he leans over, gets within six inches of my face and starts laughing at the top of his lungs, along with the other two monkeys with him. He tells me that he's no thief. He's a businessman and that's why I need to deal with him, and only him."

"So what about your friend who introduced you to him?" the agent asked.

"We left the motel and he apologized all the way back to his place. We got the shipments up and running. Everything worked like clockwork. Then one day his wife gives me a panic call in the middle of the day. Poor bastard went out for a carton of milk for their kid and never came back. Here one day, gone the next. That was the last time his wife saw him. Really creepy!"

"How so?" the agent asked.

"Because he was the one who warned me not to even *think* about screwing this guy. Don't miss a payment. That I'd be dead or missing in a heartbeat. He knew about a couple of dealers that were greased by this guy for skimming money."

"So what do you think your friend did to get on the wrong side of this guy?"

"I can't imagine," Millner said.

"Tell you what, we'll sit on your condo and have you shadowed until this deal gets wrapped up. We're going to wire your place. When are they supposed to contact you about another shipment?"

"The next couple of days," Millner confirmed to the agent.

"Good, then maybe we can bust them when they bring the shipment in and find our Colombian at the same time. I'll call Miami and see if they can help us find this guy."

"In the meantime, I am supposed to do what?" the dealer asked indignantly.

"You are supposed to go on with life like nothing has happened," the agent bellowed. "Don't worry. We'll be in the neighborhood."

"Great! That's reassuring," Millner scoffed.

Chapter Forty

DEA HEADQUARTERS, MIAMI – 9:45 PM

The phone buzzed on the agent's desk and he ran to get to it. "Hello, this is Agent Guzman speaking."

"Agent Guzman, my name is Thomas Gibbs, Cincinnati DEA office."

"I didn't know DEA even had an office there," Guzman said.

"Well, the truth is, we are a small office. Kind of flying under the radar screen so to speak. Tiny compared to you guys down there where they're selling on every corner."

"You got that right. What can I do for you, Agent Gibbs?"

"During the course of a bust up here today we got information about a cocaine distribution network that originates out of Miami. The guy we took down couldn't give us a name but said he was major dealer, probably from South America. Can your office send me any information or pictures of guys that would fit that profile? Maybe our guy can identify one of your surveillance photos."

"Sure, I'll check the files and send you up everyone we're looking at in our database. If he's shipping from here to Ohio he's definitely a major player," Guzman said.

"That's what the guy we busted said, too. He thought maybe he was ex-military. A real bad ass."

"Appreciate the call. I'll start digging around and send you what we have."

Guzman hung up the phone and sat there for a moment with an absent smile.

"What was that all about?" Guzman's chief asked.

"That was a DEA agent from Cincinnati. He wanted to know if we're looking at anyone running a distribution network up to the Midwest. I wonder if our two mules that we lost today are involved," the agent asked rhetorically.

"By the way boss, did Rodriquez or Davis get back with the phone records from the guy who lives over in Coconut Grove?"

"I believe the answer is yes," McPherson said. The two agents walked into the office with folders in hand.

"We dumped his land line but couldn't find a cell phone provider who had a listing under his name or address," Davis said as he handed Guzman the files.

The agent looked over the files. "A lot of in bound calls from the same couple of numbers. You guys start running them down and give me the names and locations that come up the most. We have to find out where Estacio is. One more thing, I need you guys to run down his credit cards. See where he bought gas, ate, stayed, anything that was charged to his credit card. I need the whole package including any bank accounts."

"We're on it," Rodriquez said.

"Did the search of the house turn up anything?" McPherson asked Guzman.

"Nah, that's why I sent them to the phone company after they searched the home. Estacio's life must be buried in his PDA, if he has one, and we didn't find it. His computer was a dead end too. The boys downstairs didn't find anything on his hard drive."

"Keep me up to speed," Mc Person told him.

"Oh, before I forget, I got a call from DOJ in Washington yesterday. They are investigating that senator's killing. They got a lead on the shooter, and they sent me a photo to see if he was in our database," Mc Person said.

"Did you get any hits?" Guzman said.

"No, he wasn't in our database, but Miami Dade had him on film. He's Estacio's partner, the guy you photographed with the customs agent. Now we have a name to go with the face. Carlos Batista."

"No shit," Guzman said as his eyes got bigger. "You think the cocaine network and the senator's murder are tied in?"

"Looks that way, Justice is sending a couple of guys down here, and they want us to join them."

"Yeah, that works," Guzman affirmed. We'll keep looking for Estacio and Batista. Maybe we can round them up when the next shipment arrives."

"Speaking of shipments, Osborne was supposed to call me as soon as he got to his house, and he didn't," the agent winced.

Guzman dialed the number and after several failed attempts slammed the phone down.

"What's wrong?" McPherson asked.

"Nobody's picking up. Dammit! This isn't good. Too much of a coincidence after today. Boss, can you get some bodies over there ASAP and find out what's going on?"

"I'll get Davis and Rodriquez on it."

Chapter Forty-One

LIME INN-ST. JOHN, USVI - 9:45 PM

"Thanks for the dinner Mr. Harper. Over the top meal," Kevin Henry told his boss.

"I'm glad the three of us could get together. I make it a point to eat here every time I come down. This place is what an island restaurant ought to be. It's quaint, the food's great and the prices are cheaper than in Florida."

"Did everybody enjoy their dinner?" the owner asked as he stood next to their table.

"Rich, you out did yourself. We all had the Caribbean lobster. Out of this world!"

"Good, I'm glad you guys enjoyed the meal. Mr. Harper, can I get you guys an after dinner drink, compliments of the house?"

"Absolutely, Rich."

"How about the specialty of the house, a Bailey's Banana Colada. It's our signature drink. Does that work for everybody?"

"Sounds good to me." Kevin and Paul answered.

"Then its three BBC's," the owner said as he went over to the bar.

"I love this place," Harper said, leaning back in the soft wicker chair. "If I were ever going to move to the islands, St. John would be it. You're still in the states, but you're a million miles removed from all the bullshit back home. It takes bucks to live here, but the cost of living other than the housing isn't outrageous. The climate, the scenery, the women, this place has it all. And it's more relaxed than St. Bart's, St. Martin, and Barbados."

"You're dead-on about this place Mr. Harper. Paul and I spent the day snorkeling on one of the beaches on the back side called Salt Pond. The water was so clear that we could see down thirty feet to the bottom. We had lunch in Coral Bay at Skinny Legs, great burgers. Everybody we met all day was incredibly friendly, especially when we asked the locals for directions," Kevin told Harper.

"The West Indians who live here are some of the nicest people you'll ever meet in your life. It's not like that on every island. The tradeoff for coming here is that you are staying on a rock, with no golf or gambling. Tennis, eating, drinking, and sex are the only non-beach activities here, which is what makes St. John so desirable. This place makes you relax. Nothing but sun, sand and water."

A waiter brought their drinks over to the table and Kevin lifted his glass up, toasting the owner.

"So, are we leaving tomorrow or the next day, Mr. Harper?" the pilot asked after he took a taste.

"I plan on spending at least another day here unless you guys have some burning desire to get back to Sarasota. A little R&R is good for the soul."

"That works for us," Kevin said.

"If you're looking for a little action I'd recommend going to either the beach bar at Wharfside Village, across from where we picked up the Jeep, or over to Woody's. The place where all the locals were hanging out, standing in the street, when we came into town. I've got to call Ronnie and fill him in on my trip to Tortola and then I'm going back to the house. Here's some cash. This should cover your night."

"Thanks for the cash and for the dinner," Kevin said as he took the bills from his boss.

"Thank you, sir," Paul added.

"Enjoy your night."

"We will, sir."

As they left, Harper finished his drink and laid his credit card on the table. The waitress took the check and card over to the cashier as he dialed his cell phone.

"Ronnie, this is Martin, is the connection good on your end?"

"Yeah. How are things going down in the islands?" Gibson asked.

"Great. I got the accounts set up in the Caymans and Tortola. I need you to transfer at least four million over to the Cayman account tomorrow first thing in the morning. Then transfer another four million over to the Tortola account. That will help with the float. I'll email the account numbers to you tonight," Harper said.

"That shouldn't be a problem. The audit is over and no major problems came up."

"I was just going to ask you about that. Did they have any issues with our financing structure for the condominium project?" Harper asked.

"No. That wasn't an issue. They had some questions and wanted some documentation on other loans, but we had everything they wanted. Their only major complaint was that we didn't make enough loans to high-risk individuals and to businesses in questionable areas of town. A subtle hint that we red lined," Gibson sneered.

"There's a surprise. The regulatory bureaucrats in Washington have an agenda for high-risk loans that they want to shove down our throats. That's why we pay so damn much protection money to our friends in Washington. That's what bothered me so much about Bubba's situation," Harper lamented.

"What are we going to do about that?"

"I'm not sure Ronnie. Murphy and Bubba weren't the same kind of people. Even though we worked with Murphy in the past, our contact guy will be the new head of the Ways and Means Committee. Money talks! Hopefully when we show the new guy how much will be coming his way, he'll bite. That's the only shot we have," Harper suggested.

"You handled that end of the business and the program always worked well," Gibson said.

"Here's hoping we can get back in the driver's seat again," Harper replied. "I have to go to Washington next week and meet with Murphy. Find out whose palm I'm going to have to grease."

"Are you coming back here tomorrow?"

"No, we're flying back on Saturday. It's nice down here. The boys and I are going to hang out for another day and take in the island life. I rented a killer villa off Centerline Road that sits a thousand feet above the water. The only thing I'm missing right now is a woman, and who knows, I may still get lucky tonight."

"Martin, you dog, you'll never change, old buddy."

"Got that right. I'm too old and too set in my ways," Harper chuckled. "Besides, there are a lot of beautiful women down here looking for a little fun. I'd be surprised if Kevin and Paul don't come back to the villa with some of the local talent. Hell, I'm going to if I can."

"Oh, before I hang up, anything strange with David?" Harper asked.

"No. He was in before the auditors got here and couldn't have been nicer. Seemed like he was in a great mood."

"Good. I'll give you the lowdown on the deal down in the islands when I get back."

Chapter Forty-Two

GULFCOAST BANK - FRIDAY 9:00 AM

"Operator, I would like to speak to someone in the Criminal Fraud Division, please," David Dreyer said in a hushed tone.

"May I have your name, sir?"

"My name is David Dreyer."

"Thank you. Can you hang on for a minute while I connect you with the agent in charge?" the operator asked.

"Yes, I will." Dreyer flipped a pen between his fingers and glanced out his window.

The voice on the other end said, "Hello, this is Agent Tullis. Who am I speaking with?"

"Agent Tullis, my name is David Dreyer. I'm calling from my office at Gulfcoast Bank in Sarasota. I'm an officer of the bank and I have some vital information for you. I want to meet with you today, the sooner the better. It has to be a secure location. I can drive up to Tampa, or we can meet somewhere in between."

"What do you want to talk to us about that is so urgent?"

"I have information that will prove that officials at this bank are involved in a conspiracy involving money laundering and fraud," the banker said.

The agent paused a few seconds to confer with someone, then told him, "Why don't we meet at the Hyatt up on 41 south of the airport? I can be there in about an hour."

Dreyer looked at his watch and grimaced, "I guess that will work."

"I'll have another agent with me. We'll be wearing dark blue blazers and tan slacks. Let's meet in the ground level restaurant, and we'll figure out where to go from there. Are you going to be all right til then?"

"Yeah, that will work. Look, I can't stay on the line any longer. I have to go. I'll be wearing a blue pinstripe suit with an open collared blue shirt. I'll be waiting for you inside the restaurant."

He ended the call and slid his cell phone into his suit coat that was hanging on the back of his chair. When he looked up, Ronnie Gibson knocked on the glass door and came in his office.

"Do you want a donut and some coffee? I stopped at the bakery on the way in."

Dreyer took a deep breath and regained his composure, "No thanks Ronnie, I had a cup of coffee before I left the house."

"Suit yourself, but these are my favorite butter donuts from Virginia Bakery."

"Oh, what the hell, I love donuts and they're the best in town."

He grabbed a glazed donut from the box, took a bite out of it and walked back to his desk. Gibson grinned like he had just closed another deal and ambled down the hall to his office. Dreyer took another bite, threw the donut in his trash can and covered it with some papers. Gibson was right, it did taste great. But the last thing he wanted to do was waste precious time talking to him. So he'd taken the path of least resistance to get rid of him.

Dreyer had a printout and a spreadsheet on his desk listing all the information he had collected from Gibson's computer. Information on Thomas Vasquez, and the dummy corporations that had been set up to launder his money. He slid them inside his briefcase and locked up his desk drawer.

That done, the banker rang his secretary. He told her to cancel all his morning appointments. He checked his watch. His feet and legs began bouncing up and down. His stomach was in knots and he still had a half an hour to kill.

"Screw it, I'm out of here," he said in exasperation.

He snatched his coat off the chair and hit the light switch on his way out of the office. Dreyer leaned into the doorway of Gibson's office and said, "Great donut Ronnie, thanks."

Gibson looked over his bifocals, lowered his Wall Street Journal, and shot back, "I knew you'd love it."

"Be back in a couple of hours."

Gibson focused back on his newspaper and waved his hand.

Dreyer hustled out the door to his car, hit the remote button and unlocked the door. He laid his briefcase on the bucket seat across from him and plopped down. He turned the ignition key, did a quick 180 and sped away.

Dreyer yanked off his tie and tossed it on top of the briefcase, then hit the max button on the air conditioner. He was feeling a bit paranoid and more than a little anxious. He reminded himself that in a couple of hours his part of the ordeal would be finished. The first step, setting up the meeting was history. Painful though it might be, he had no alternative. He always did what was right. The only thing his conscience would allow him to do. Dreyer had grown up with a set of values that couldn't be compromised.

As he waited for the light to change at Stickney Point Road and 41, a sense of anxiety began to overwhelm him. He fought it off by taking shallow breaths, by flashing back to better days at the beach and on the boat with his family.

He undid another button on his shirt, rolled down his window and looked across the street at the palm trees swaying in the breeze. The clean smell of saltwater rushed into the car. A sense of calm enveloped him. Life for him and his family would go on. It was going to be a struggle, but they were going to make it.

Chapter Forty-Three

PALM ISLAND CLUB OF SARASOTA - 9:30 AM

"Is Tomas there?" Carlos Batista asked in a nervous tone.

"Yes he is, hold on for a second."

Elena Vasquez handed her husband the phone and continued reading her newspaper.

"Boss, our man contacted the feds. He's gonna meet them this morning up at the Hyatt. We were on our way down to your place when we picked Dreyer's conversation up from the bug in his office."

He jumped up from the table, opened the balcony door and stepped quickly. "I knew that guy would be a problem for us. Where are you now?"

"On 41, we just passed the Phillipi Creek," Batista said.

"Listen up, you guys are about a mile from the bank. Stay on the line while I call the bank on my cell to see if he's still in his office. Take him out in the parking lot if you have to, just get him!"

Vasquez set the phone down on the glass table and called the bank. "Ronnie, this is Tomas. Is David still in his office?"

"No, he just walked out the door. Why?" Gibson asked as he sat his newspaper down.

"Did Dreyer drive the green Lexus today?"

"Yeah, why?" he demanded, a sinking feeling in his stomach.

"I have to see him right away. Do you know where he was headed?"

"No, he told me he would be back later. I can check with his secretary and see what his morning schedule looks like," Gibson offered.

"Yeah, do that. I'll hold on." Vasquez put his hand over the receiver and raged, "That bastard knows we're on to him."

A couple of seconds later Gibson was back on the other end of the line. "He cancelled all of his morning appointments. I have no idea where he's headed."

"Call me the minute that son-of-a-bitch contacts you," Vasquez ordered.

"Will do Thomas, but what's going on?" Gibson asked fearing the answer.

Vasquez tossed his cell down on the plastic patio table and picked up the land line.

"Carlos, he just left the office. He's driving a dark green Lexus 430. Turn around and head north on 41. If you spot him on the highway, force him over. You have to stop him any way you can. I don't care if you have to take him out in the parking lot of the Hyatt."

"Understood, boss! Pedro is pointing across the street. A dark green Lexus just made the turn onto 41. I'm at the light. I'll make a U-turn and be on him."

"Keep the line open, I'm on my way. As soon as you catch up with him force him off the road, or get into his car. Do whatever it takes. After you get him drive his car to the nearest side street, and let me know where you are. I'll meet up with you and we will dispose of him and the car," he raged.

"I'll be on the car in thirty seconds. I just passed a Chevy dealership across from a shopping mall. Traffic is stopped for the light and Pedro is getting out of the car."

Dreyer pressed the button on his cell phone as fast as his stubby little fingers would allow.

"Come on, come on, pick up, Sarah!"

"David?"

"Sarah, listen up. You have to get out of the house, and don't come back until you hear from me again. The thirty eight is in the console. Just Go! Go! Get out of there now! I'll explain later."

He switched the phone off before she could answer and dropped it between the console and his seat. He saw something out of the corner of his eye. A figure in the car next to his, gesturing at him. He didn't look over until the passenger side window rolled all the way down, and he heard the man screaming at him in an agitated voice. Then he saw the gun pointed at him and lurched back in the seat. His heart was in his mouth. He waited for the shot, but there wasn't one. He inched forward and looked up at the light praying for it to change, but it didn't. He was boxed in. No where to go.

The driver continued screaming at him and motioned with the gun. He wanted Dreyer to wind his window down. The light turned green and the car ahead of him began to move. That was followed by a knock on the passenger side window that startled him. Another man was standing there in traffic, banging on the passenger side window with a gun. It was do or die time. He had a nanosecond to act. By the time he did it was too late. Horns were blaring behind both cars, but only he could see the weapons. Nobody was going to help him. He lowered his window, and the driver in the other car screamed out. "My trigger finger is faster than your foot."

Dreyer looked over at the man by his passenger window, one might miss him, but both wouldn't.

"Don't do it," the driver screamed. "Open the door for my partner. I'm not going to say it again," the thug yelled as he pulled the hammer back on his handgun.

Dreyer unlocked the passenger door, and the driver's partner sat down with the gun pointed at him. "Now you can go, senor."

The banker pressed the pedal and the car moved.

"Drive slowly so my friend has no problem following you," Estacio told him as he pointed the nine millimeter at him.

"We got him, boss," Batista yelled in the cell phone.

"Good work, Carlos."

"Look for Hane's Furniture Store. It will be on your left. Take the first street after that on the right hand side of the road, and stop half way down the block. I'll be there in five minutes," Vasquez said.

Chapter Forty-Four

___

WASHINGTON D.C. – 9:30 AM

Charlie Brune had a smirk on his face as his investigators arrived for their morning meeting.

"You look like the cat that just ate the canary," Trupp told him as he placed his coffee down next to his folder.

"Try this on for size. I called the DEA office in Miami yesterday afternoon to see if they had any new information for us. Agent Guzman told me that the photo of Batista I sent down matched the picture he had of a Colombian they were looking at in a smuggling operation. A few minutes after that confirmation took place he got a call from their Cincinnati office. They were inquiring about a major cocaine dealer operating out of Miami, shipping product into the Midwest. The guy they busted met the head guy," he told his men.

"So where's the connection to our case?" Trupp asked.

"Right now all we have is that they're Colombians. It just so happens that Vasquez is too. Given the fact that his company is a Panamanian subsidiary, and he banks with Harper, maybe he should be the guy we focus on. Maybe this whole probe is about distribution of drugs and money laundering," Brune said.

"Sounds to me like the key link in the chain is the guy they busted in Cincinnati who can identify the ring leader. If you're right Charlie, we can short circuit the whole process by getting a picture of Vasquez and send it down to Miami for confirmation. Ms. Boudreaux might be able to help us in that department. I'll give her a call," Herzog said as he reached for his cell phone.

He dialed her number, hoping his friends wouldn't pick up on their budding relationship. "Adrienne, this is Richard, how are you doing?"

"It's getting a little better every day. Thank you for asking."

"Glad to hear that. I wonder if you could help us out one more time," Herzog paused. He got up and moved away from the other agents.

"Sure, what can I do?" she asked cheerily.

"When you were packing up Senator Harrington's belongings, do you remember coming across a picture of Thomas Vasquez anywhere? I thought maybe since he was such a large contributor there might be a picture of him and the senator hanging around."

Adrienne thought for a moment and said, "As a matter of fact I did. The senator used to keep a picture of himself, Mr. Harper and Mr. Vasquez on his desk. It was from a golf outing down in Florida. The Senator told me he had a hole-in-one, and they took a picture of the three of them standing next to the flag stick on the green."

"Great. Do you still have it in the office?" Herzog pleaded.

"I do. It's packed up. But I'll dig it out for you."

"Thanks, Adrienne. I'll be over in a flash to pick it up." A hint of a smile crossed Herzog's face before he turned around and went back to the desk.

"I'll have it for you when you arrive," she told him. Herzog put the phone back in his pocket and sat down.

"So you are on a first name basis now?" Trupp chided him.

"We are. She's a nice lady who's caught up in a real shit storm. The fact is she's helped us out a lot. It's just business between us though," Herzog said, pleading his case.

"Rich, why don't you go now and get the photograph. As soon as you get back we'll send it out to the folks in Cincinnati and Miami, and you guys can head down to Sarasota," Brune told him.

"I want you there ASAP. Harper's bank is the focal point. When you get there, the first thing to check out is Caribbean Ventures. Based on the information we have I can get authorization for taps on the Vasquez house and a look at his phone records, credit cards and bank statements," the agent assured his men.

"My bags are packed and in the car. We can leave as soon as I get back," Herzog said. He grabbed his files and headed out the door.

"That's fine with me," Trupp added. "I have my gear sitting in the office. We can swing by and pick it up on the way to Reagan. That will give me time to make a few phone calls here while I wait for Rich to get back."

Brune nodded. "I'll start rounding up blanket subpoenas and the wiretaps you guys are going to need when you get to Florida."

Chapter Forty-Five

_____

SARASOTA HYATT – 10:30 AM

The two FBI agents followed a couple of elderly patrons into the first floor restaurant area and scanned the room. Groups of people were clustered about the circular tables. They saw a couple of business types dressed in tan and beige suits, but nobody fitting the description of the caller was in the room.

"Would you gentlemen like a table this morning?" the hostess asked.

Tullis turned towards her, opened his wallet and showed his badge. His partner, Agent Honner did the same.

"How can I help you gentlemen?"

"Have you been here all morning?" Honner asked.

"Since seven."

"Did you see a man dressed in a blue pinstriped suit and a blue shirt with an open collar in here this morning?"

"No sir, I did not," she answered.

"What about outside in the lobby area?"

"No sir, we don't offer service there in the morning."

The agent looked at his watch and grimaced.

"Dammit, he only had a twenty minute drive. He should have been here by now," Tullis mumbled.

The waitress gave him a strange look but didn't say anything.

"Tell you what, we're going to sit over at that table by the window that overlooks the parking lot," Honner told her.

"That would be fine. Go ahead and seat yourself. I'll have some coffee and water sent over to you."

"That would be good," Honner said. The agents strolled over and sat down.

"I don't like the feeling in the pit of my stomach," Tullis said. "This guy sounded desperate. There's no way in hell that he shouldn't have been here by now." Tullis eyes wondered around the room as he spoke.

"The fact that he didn't show up after basically begging me to meet him tells me we have a major problem."

"Did we get his number or the branch location he was calling from?" Honner asked.

"No we didn't. The guy told me he was on a cell phone, and he didn't stay on the phone long enough for me to get that information. He was really spooked."

"I'll call the office and have Karey pull his number from the phone log, and have the provider run down the address for us," Honner said.

He pulled his cell phone from his jacket pocket and called their assistant. "Karey, this is Ed. We have to run a trace on the call Mark got this morning. Our guy didn't show up and we have to find him. Any chance he called back?"

"No, I haven't taken any calls since you guys left," his assistant told him.

"Karey, find the number and the provider, as well as his billing address and call me back as soon as you get it."

A couple of minutes later Honner's cell phone rang.

"Agent Honner, it's Karey."

"What do you have?"

"His number is 941-701-5074. The provider lists the billing address as 1100 Bay Shore Lane, Sarasota," she told him.

"We know he works at Gulfcoast Bank, my guess is that he works at the corporate headquarters. We need that address too."

"Yes, sir, I'll get back to you with that," his assistant told him.

"No luck on his work location?" Tullis asked.

"Not yet, but we have his cell number and the billing address, which also lists a Mrs. Maybe she can shed some light on what's going on, or where he might have gone. I'll try his cell and see if he answers. If we strike out there, then maybe we should go to the house," Honner said.

He punched in the number and let it ring a dozen times before he hit the off button.

"No go, he isn't picking up."

"As of now he's officially a missing person. Ed, why don't you buzz Karey back and get directions to the house? I'll run down the hostess and give her our card on the off chance that he shows up later. I'll meet you out in the lobby," a dejected Tullis told his partner.

Chapter Forty-Six

D.O.J. OFFICE, WASHINGTON D.C.-11:00 AM

"You made good time getting back from Harrington's office," Brune told his agent. "I'll have the lab downstairs enhance the picture of Vasquez and send it out to Miami and Cincinnati."

"I'm ready to head over to Reagan. Where are our travel vouchers?" Herzog asked.

"There's been a change in plans. I was able to get you guys a ride on the company plane. So get your butts over to Andrews Air Force Base. They're waiting for you," Brune instructed.

"Made my day Charlie," Trupp said as he reached across the desk and high fived him.

"Ditto Charlie. I hate to fly anymore with all the bullshit you have to go through at the airport," Herzog groused.

"I had an ulterior motive. You guys can be on the ground two hours sooner and go right to the bank."

"What about our subpoenas?" Herzog asked.

The lead agent lifted them from his desk and slapped them in Trupp's hands. "They're for the bank and the residences and all personal property of

Harper and Vasquez. It also covers Caribbean Ventures, Vasquez' holding company."

"What about wire taps," Herzog pressed his boss.

"I couldn't get them for their personal residences with the same judge. But I have somebody in mind who will issue them for us, provided I can locate him. If it works out I should have them by the time you land in Sarasota.

Brune reached into the side of his desk and pulled out a handgun and a shoulder holster along with a DOJ badge. "Rich, here's a nine millimeter. I assume you remember how to use it."

"Sure, but do you think I'll need it?" the agent asked, a surprised look on his face. Herzog took the gun and looked it over. Then he put it inside the holster and slid it inside his brief case.

"Absolutely. You guys don't know what's going to happen once you get down there. I want you to have the freedom to take these guys down by yourselves if need be. My first choice is for the FBI agents to do it," Brune postured to his agents.

"Who's running the show, the FBI agents?" Trupp asked.

"No way," Brune emphasized. "This agency is running the show. I'll call the Tampa bureau and coordinate everything between you guys, DEA and them. Rich, you and Russell are calling the shots."

"How do you want us to proceed once we get there?" Herzog asked.

"Your first priority is to track the money flow through that bank. I'm guessing Caribbean Ventures is the tip of the iceberg. See if they were laundering money through that company. There has to be somebody besides Harper at that bank who knows what's going on. When you find out who that person is, put the screws to him. Threaten him with anything and everything to get cooperation."

"I'm glad we've got carte blanche to go after these people, Charlie," Trupp said as he got up and headed to the door.

"Damn, this feels strange carrying a gun again, and thinking about the prospect of having to use it," Herzog said.

"It's just like riding a bike. It will all come back if you have to use it," Brune assured him.

"You guys be careful."

"Count on that," Trupp said.

.

Chapter Forty-Seven

SARASOTA - 11:30 AM

Tullis and Honner pulled into the paver stone driveway of the sprawling, beige colored Mediterranean house. The garage door was open, but the cars were gone. Tullis slid out from behind the wheel and pulled his Glock 40 caliber out of his holster. Honner did the same and slipped around the side of the house with his weapon drawn. When he got to the pool area in the back, he tugged open the screen door to the covered lanai and checked out the inside of the house.

Tullis inched across the front perimeter of the house, and peered into the windows. When he reached the front door he pounded repeatedly, but there was no response.

Honner came back to the front of the house from the opposite side. "Did you see any activity inside the house through the front windows?"

"No. What about you?"

"Zip." Honner said.

Both agents stood there with a befuddled look on their faces.

"All the exterior doors to the house are locked, and the garage door is wide open?" Tullis wondered.

"This isn't the kind of house you leave open in broad daylight. Even though it's a gated community and security is probably good here, there's always service guys working in the area. Whoever was here left in a hurry," Honner speculated.

"This guy doesn't meet us like he was supposed to; then his wife hauls ass out of here at the same time," Tullis declared.

The agents pounded on the entry door to the house but got no response. They went back into the garage with guns drawn. Tullis twisted the handle on the entry door. He pushed it back and they went inside. A half filled cup of coffee and a partially eaten piece of toast were on the glass top kitchen table. The television set in the family room was turned on. They searched every room in the house and ended up back in the kitchen a few minutes later.

"This can't be good," Tullis said.

They walked out through the garage and sauntered back to their car. Tullis started issuing orders as he turned the ignition key. "Ed, call the office and have Karey dump the phone lines for the house, and see if she has a cell. See who either of them talked to this morning, and have both of them listed as missing persons."

Honner called to relay the instructions to their assistant. He listened to her for a couple of seconds and spoke again. "Thanks for the update— and Karey, Mark wants you to list both the husband and wife as missing persons." Honner ended the call and looked at Tullis.

"Hang on a minute Mark, it's Karey again."

The agent pressed his cell button and listened while their admin relayed instruction to him. "So we are to rendezvous with them at the airport and proceed from there. Got it."

"What's going on?" Tullis asked.

"DOJ is sending a team down from Washington to go after the principals of Gulfcoast Bank. DEA is also involved. Our instructions are to join them at Sarasota airport and proceed together."

"No shit?"

"That's the word from the top. I wonder how Dreyer is tied into all of this?"

"I guess we'll find out when they get here. You did say DEA was also involved," Tullis asked.

"I did. This is a hell of a lot more than a little bank fraud case," Honner said.

"Let's head for the airport. My curiosity is killing me, on more than one front," Tullis answered.

"We should have the security guard at the gate check the camera on the way out. See when she left," Honner suggested.

"At least that will be a start," Tullis said.

Chapter Forty-Eight

DEA HEADQUARTERS, MIAMI- 12:00 PM

"I just heard from the Cincinnati office," Guzman blurted out. "The guy they busted up there the other day positively identified the photo sent over from Justice. Thomas Vasquez is the guy we should be looking at. We can't put Batista and Vasquez together yet, but it sure looks like a good fit."

"So where is the connection?" McPherson asked.

"Brune from DOJ told me that Vasquez has business interests in Sarasota and Miami. It's too much of a coincidence that he and Batista came into the country from Colombia about the same time. Given that he's a drug dealer who also happens to be on the radar screen in the Harrington murder case, it looks like it's all connected," the agent speculated.

"So how does he want us to proceed?" the senior agent asked.

"He has two investigators on the way down to Sarasota. He'd like me to hook up with them and bring the surveillance photos of Estacio and Batista. He thinks Vasquez could still be in Sarasota."

"If the Department of Justice wants you up in Sarasota, get your butt on the next plane and join them. Rodriquez and Davis can cover the action down here."

"Anything on our informant, Osborne?"

"Not a trace. He and his wife are gone," McPherson informed him.

"Dammit! I should have never given in to him and let him return to the house to pick up food and clothes, even though it was his off day. I should have done it myself, especially after yesterday. I screwed up big time," the agent lamented.

McPherson shook his head back and forth a couple of times. "Jorge, you can't beat yourself up about this. Davis and Rodriquez checked everything out, and there were no signs of a struggle. And their car hasn't been located either. Hell, maybe he's gone into hiding, or maybe he's got a safe house with some relative somewhere," McPherson said, trying to put a positive spin on a bad situation.

Guzman shrugged his shoulders. "Boss, I need the photo of Vasquez to take with me, if that's OK. You got another copy, right?"

"Get out of here," McPherson told Guzman as he handed him the manila envelope containing the Colombian's photograph. The agent slung his coat over his shoulder and hustled out of the office.

The metal gate rolled back, and Guzman flew out of the lot onto A1A. He kept thinking what an emotional roller coaster the past couple of days had been. Maybe his luck was about to change. The glimmer of hope was based on the photograph he had and the fact that he could identify Batista and Estacio.

As he shot in and out of traffic trying to beat every light to the airport, his imagination began to run wild. How was his case related to theirs, and vice versa? A key piece to the puzzle was right in front of him. *Nail Vasquez and you get all the answers*, he told himself.

Chapter Forty-Nine

ST. THOMAS AIRPORT, USVI -1:00 PM

The Gulfstream roared down the asphalt sending rooster-tails of water into the air. Rain pelted the windshield reducing visibility to a couple of hundred feet. As they approached the windsock at the end of the runway, the jet's nose lifted off the runway as the wings grabbed lift. Climbing sharply, the plane banked at a forty-five degree angle to the right as soon as it achieved the proper altitude.

A couple of minutes later the craft leveled out on the easterly heading. They climbed slowly through the cloud bank until they reached 5,000 feet, the plane turned again, heading north and resumed its climb until it reached an altitude of 20,000 feet. They passed over the southern shore of the island of Culebra.

"I'm sorry about the hasty departure guys, but I couldn't see staying down here to look at it rain all day," Harper said through his speaker phone back in the passenger cabin.

"Not a problem sir. The plane was ready to go and so were Paul and I. We should be out of this tropical depression by the time we pass over San

Salvador, and should have a great ride up to
Sarasota," his pilot told him.

"Thanks for the update."

As soon as he turned off the speaker phone,
the satellite phone next to him rang.

"Ronnie, I'm surprised to hear from you,"
Harper answered. "What's up?"

"I've been trying to get ahold of you for the
past two hours. I called the house, your cell and
eventually the plane. You must have been on your
way to the airport."

"We were. What's up?"

"We got a problem. Thomas called this
morning in a panic asking if David was still in the
office. I could tell from the tone of his voice he was
pissed. He didn't say why he wanted to see him but
told me he had to see him right away."

"Did he tell you what was so urgent?"

"No, David had been in earlier and told me
he'd be back in a couple of hours. I checked with
Jeanie, and she told me he cancelled all of his
morning appointments," Gibson said, trying to catch
his breath.

"So what did you tell Thomas?"

"What I just told you, and he hung up. So I
called back to his condo and Elena told me he got a
call earlier and stormed out of the apartment. I don't
have a clue what's going on."

Harper's face went crimson, and he got a
hollow feeling in the pit of his stomach.

"Did David act odd this morning, like
something was bothering him?"

"No, not at all. He even had one of my donuts
from Virginia Bakery before he left the office. Told me
he'd be back in a couple of hours," Gibson repeated.

"Let me guess. You haven't been able to
reach him on his cell phone either?"

"Nope."

Harper didn't say anything for a few seconds while he mulled over what Gibson had told him. He had to get to the bottom of this but couldn't do it over the phone with Gibson.

"Ronnie, let me call you back in a couple of minutes. I'll try and get ahold of Sarah. Maybe she knows where he's at," Harper said timidly.

"That's fine. I'll wait for your call."

Harper hung up and frantically pressed the number for his daughter's house. It rang until the answering machine kicked in. He tried her cell and struck out there too. Harper pressed the end button and stared out the window for a couple of minutes. His son-in-law's vanishing act coupled with his inability to reach his daughter were bad omens for him. He didn't believe in coincidences at, least not where his family was concerned. He made a snap judgment and called Gibson back.

"Ronnie, this is Martin again."

"Any luck with your daughter?"

"No." Harper said with a fatal tone. "Ronnie, it sounds like Thomas has gone off of the deep end. Here's what I need you to do. Let's make sure we get some of the excess cash out of the bank. If the Brinks courier truck hasn't been there yet, increase the transfer amount to the University Park branch by one million dollars. The next step is to wire transfer the remainder of the money in the dummy corporation to the new account at Banco Nationale. We'll park it down there for a couple of days, then move it to Zurich later on."

"The courier is here now. I can fill out the papers and have the extra million sent out with the rest of the cash going out to the branches," Gibson confirmed.

"That's perfect. Make sure they go to University Park first. After it gets deposited and you

make the wire transfer, call me back," Harper
instructed.

"I'll do the electronic transfers as soon as I get
the cash shipment out. But why move all the money
around right now?"

"Because it sounds like Thomas has gone off
the reservation. And he sure as hell doesn't need to
know how or where we're moving all the money. If he
comes in or calls, tell him it's all been wired to
Zurich," Harper snapped.

"The Cayman transfer should be done within
half an hour. I'll touch base with you when I get it all
wrapped up," Gibson promised.

Harper signed off and reached inside his
briefcase. He pulled out his black book and flipped
the pages until he found all his bank account
numbers. He scoured his brain but couldn't fathom
why Vasquez had gone ballistic, or why David was
the object of his rage.

Until he landed in Sarasota his only option was
to play defense, try and stay one step ahead. Thirty
minutes passed and he decided to call Banco
Nationale in the Cayman Islands.

"Geoffrey, this is Martin Harper. You're
probably surprised to hear from me so soon."

"Always good to hear from you, Mr. Harper,"
Parsons said. "How can I help you?"

"I need access to some cash for a property
purchase that literally just came up. Can you transfer
four million from Gulf and Bay Enterprises to my
personal account in Abaco today?"

"Yes, I can do that as soon as I can verify the
account balance. Do you have the numbers handy?"

"The Gulf and Bay number is 375- 892-5130.
The account number in Abaco is 775-541-4540. I will
also need you to transfer four million dollars to your
branch in Tortola. My account number there is 790-
775-9983."

"Very good, sir. I will put the information in the computer, check the deposit base and make the wire transfer. I see the account balance is sufficient to accommodate your request, but the wire transfer may take a little while. Let me get that started and I'll get back with you in a minute or so."

Harper stared out the window again, gazing down to the cobalt blue water below, fixing his gaze on the specks of islands that dotted the seascape. His concentration was broken by a voice on the other end.

"Mr. Harper, are you there?"

"Yes Geoffrey, go ahead."

"With the transfer of funds today, you have a balance of two million US in the Gulf and Bay account. If you think you are going to need more than that I can extend you a line of credit," the Cayman banker told him.

"I appreciate that Geoffrey, but with the transfer I think I have enough to cover my immediate needs," Harper said. Relieved that there was still a significant balance in the account that he could tap later if need be, and that Parsons hadn't raised any red flags about the withdrawals

"It was good hearing from you again, sir. Have a safe trip back."

"Thanks again for your help Geoffrey. I'll give you a call next week."

A couple of minutes later Ronnie Gibson called back and confirmed the money transfers. Harper hung up and waited a couple of minutes before he called Lionel Smith, the Banco Nationale manager in Tortola.

"Mr. Smith, Martin Harper. I didn't think we would be speaking to each other so soon, but I need to transfer some funds."

"Nice to hear from you again, Mr. Harper. Give me the specifics and we will get right on it."

"I would like you to transfer four million in U.S. currency from account number 790-775-9983 to my account at Bahamian Island Bank in Abaco. My account number there is 775-541-4540," Harper said.

"This transaction may take a little while, but it will be complete by the end of the business day if not before. How would you like confirmation of the transfer? Paper, email?"

"No, that won't be necessary. We're very informal at Gulfcoast. A phone call is sufficient. I'm in transit anyway. So how about letting me call you back?"

"If that is your wish sir," Smith told him.

"Will the work be completed by 5:00 p.m.?"

"Absolutely. That's plenty of time," the banker assured him.

"Then count on my call at 5:00 p.m. sharp."

"I will expect to hear from you then. A pleasure doing business with you, Mr. Harper."

"As well, Mr. Smith."

Harper tossed the black book back into his briefcase and speculated about the turmoil unfolding back in Sarasota. With every passing minute his blood pressure rose, and not just because of his son-in-law. The plight of his daughter was weighing on him as well. Was she in trouble too? Were both of them on the run? And back to the core issue of the day, why was Vasquez acting so irrational?

He knew from day one that there was a measured level of risk with his banking operations – in particular, the relationship he had with Thomas Vasquez. That's why he micromanaged as much as he did, keeping everyone on a short leash. So that he could minimize any potential problems.

Now he chided himself for ignoring his instincts about his son-in-law, missing the warning signals he had been given. Everything was magnified with his greatest concern being his daughter. If Vasquez was after David Dreyer, Harper knew he couldn't intervene, especially now. The only person he could help was Sarah, provided he could locate her.

His gut told him it was time to cut his losses and get his family out of Sarasota. But that would be possible only if Thomas Vasquez was out of the picture. The weak link in the chain for him would be for the Colombian to somehow find out about the diversion of money into Harper's account and that he was flying back to Sarasota today. That's why he needed Ronnie Gibson to run interference for him with Vasquez.

Harper called back to the bank and got Gibson's secretary on the line.

"Brenda, I need to talk to Ronnie. Is he there?"

"Yes, sir, hold on please, while I get him."
Harper waited a few seconds for Gibson to pick up.

"Martin, this is Ronnie. I just got off of the phone with Thomas. He wants you and me to meet him at the marina tonight, at nine o'clock and —hold on a second, there's some commotion out in the lobby."

Harper's ear drum pounded when Gibson dropped the phone down on the desk.

"Dammit Ronnie," Harper wailed into the empty phone.

The banker came back on the line in a shrill voice. "Martin, we've got big trouble. There's a bunch of guys in suits flashing badges in the lobby. Looks like feds. I got to go."

"Ronnie, hello, hello," the line went dead. "Dammit!"

Harper ran his index finger back and forth along the base of his lip. His brain was fried. He was in limbo. What the hell could he do sitting in a plane 20,000 feet over the Caribbean?

For a control freak who always prided himself on his problem solving skills, Harper had a sudden feeling he'd met his match. A self-absorbed man, who visualized life as a game of chess, didn't feel like a player now. He felt more like a pawn or a rook.

Harper wiped the perspiration from his brow and fiddled with the air conditioner vent trying to get more cool air. The chain of events had reduced him to a voyeur, until he was able to summon the rage that boiled inside concerning his daughter. That became his focal point, along with his wife Judith. Screw everything else, he thought. He picked up the plane's intercom phone.

"Kevin, as soon as we land I want you to refuel and take the plane down to Ft. Myers. When you get there, file a flight plan for Key West. Stay on board the plane. I'll meet you down in Ft. Myers as soon as I get a couple of things straightened out. Judith is already down there. She wants to fly down to the Keys tonight instead of waiting until tomorrow."

"Not a problem sir, I'll make the arrangements," Kevin assured him.

"What can I say? I want to keep my wife happy," Harper said, unprompted.

Kevin's face contorted a bit as he looked over at his co-pilot. Paul turned and said, "Did I really hear what I think I just heard?"

Kevin raised his eyebrows and told him, "You did. That's why we're paid to fly and not to think. Go ahead and get the coordinates for Ft. Myers so that you can enter them into the computer after we land."

Back in the passenger cabin Harper pulled his black book out again and pressed in a new set of numbers.

"Judith, this is Martin."

"What's the matter dear? You sound upset," his wife said.

"It's been a long day. Have you heard from Sarah today?"

"No. Why?" his wife answered.

"I called earlier and couldn't reach her. I'll catch her later," he said, his voice trailing off.

"Judith, the other reason I'm calling is to tell you there's been a change in plans. Don't take the seven o'clock flight up from Ft. Lauderdale. Instead, meet me at the Boca Raton Airport at ten o'clock. If I'm running late I'll give you a call. I'll explain everything when I see you. We're going down to Key West for a couple of days."

"You be careful and I'll see you at ten. Goodbye, Martin."

"Bye."

Harper flipped the pages in his little black book. One last call. He dialed the number for an old island jumper pilot named Ted Moses. Moses ran a charter service that Harper had used in the past to fly him and his special cargo to the Bahamas and Cayman Islands. Trips that Gibson, Vasquez--and especially Dreyer--never knew about.

"Teddy, this is Martin Harper. How goes it?"

"Doing good, Mr. H. Haven't heard from you for a while. You need a ride?" the crafty old treetop flyer asked.

"That's why I'm calling. I need you to fly me to Abaco tonight. You always told me that you didn't book evening flights. Is that still the case?" Harper pressed.

"Yeah, I got nothing going on," the pilot told him.

"Perfect. If you do this for me tonight, I guarantee you'll have a big payday,"

"I'm always interested in big paydays. You know me," the pilot chuckled.

"Good. You have to be at Boca Raton airport gassed up and ready to go by ten o'clock. You know that Harley you were telling me that you wanted to buy? Well, tonight's trip is going to pay for it and then some."

"Ye-haa!" Moses shouted. "Sounds like a deal to me, Mr. H. The plane'll be ready to go when you get here."

"I'll be there as soon as I can," the banker said.

Harper set the phone down and reached in his brief case for his Tums. His mind began to race again. A sense of guilt began to overwhelm him, not over his actions but out of concern for his daughter and son-in-law. He should have defused the situation with Dreyer and maybe everything could have been averted.

Now there was a whole new set of problems. Why were the feds were involved, and why the eleventh hour meeting with Vasquez? If the feds pressed Gibson, Harper was confident he would give up Vasquez, not him. This would buy him the time he needed to get out of the country.

Harper looked at his Rolex. It was time to call Smith at Banco Nationale. He got the confirmation on the electronic funds transfer from Tortola to Abaco. Everything was in place, but everything wasn't right. That would happen when he heard Sarah's voice, when he knew she was out of harm's way.

Chapter Fifty

GULFCOAST BANK, SARASOTA - 3:00 PM

"Who's in charge here?" Herzog yelled out as he held his badge up in the air for everyone in the bank to see.

"I am. Who are you?" Gibson said as he bolted from his office to the lobby. Customers left the teller windows and scurried for the doors. The only people who remained were bank employees

"I'm Agent Herzog, and this is Agent Trupp." All of the agents flashed their badges in unison as if on cue.

"We're from the Department of Justice. To my right is Agent Guzman from DEA and FBI Agents Tullis and Honner. And your name is?"

"Ronnie Gibson, I'm the bank president."

"Well Mr. Gibson, it's time to lock the place down, because you are closed for business as of this minute. If you have any customers still remaining, clear them out. Have your staff remain at their stations."

Herzog slapped a paper against Gibson's chest. "Here's a search warrant to inspect every record, transaction, customer file and your hard drives. We have authority to seize all currency and impound virtually everything in this building."

Herzog looked around. "Any questions?"

"What do you want?" Gibson asked.

"For starters, David Dreyer. Where the hell is he?" Tullis raged.

"I don't know where he is. He left the bank at nine o'clock this morning, and I haven't seen or heard from him since," Gibson said with a strained look on his face.

"Let's go back to your office for a little one-on-one. Which one of these ladies is your admin?"

Gibson pointed to the lady with raven colored hair in her early twenties wearing a pink and gray business suit. Herzog motioned her to join them.

Herzog looked at the name on her lapel and told her, "Brenda, I want you to pull the records for Thomas Vasquez and his company Caribbean Ventures. Agent Guzman will accompany you."

"Yes sir," she said, leading Guzman to her office.

The three other agents followed Gibson back to his office. The banker sat down in an oversized leather chair behind the desk. The two FBI agents remained standing while Trupp sat on the corner of his oversized desk.

"Let me connect the dots for you, Mr. Gibson," Herzog began. "The FBI is involved because they were supposed to meet David Dreyer this morning, and he never showed up. The DEA is involved because Thomas Vasquez has been positively identified as the leader of a cocaine smuggling operation. The Department of Justice is involved because we believe Vasquez and his associates may have been involved in a murder plot of a government official."

"I don't know anything about any of that," Gibson shook his head.

"Did you get dropped on your head a lot when your were a little kid, or are you just another dumb ass crook in a suit? We have a missing person case, a drug distribution network, conspiracy to commit murder, and I would bet money laundering. Guess what? You're holding the winning ticket to this lottery," Herzog scoffed.

The agent pressed on, "All we have to prove is that someone at the bank, yourself for example, had knowledge of any of the illegal transactions and we can wrap it all up with a RICO charge."

Gibson looked back across the desk and slumped back into his chair, visibly shaken.

"Now, I'm guessing that Dreyer called Agent Tullis to lay out the details of your little operation here, but somebody got to him," Herzog continued. "How could that have happened?"

Gibson's eyes widened and he bit down on his lip.

"I don't know anything about David's disappearance. He was in the office this morning, and told me he was going out on a call. That he'd be back in a couple of hours."

"Tell you what. I'm going to give you one more chance to tell us everything you know, and maybe we can work out some kind of deal. I'm pointing this out to you because this offer is only on the table today, provided you come clean. But if you keep stonewalling us like you've been, then one of my guys will take you out behind this building and beat the snot out of you. Then we'll bring you back in for more questions, and the deal is history. Kapish?"

"For Chrissake you can't do that," Gibson said as his face went gaunt and gray.

"The hell I can't. Do you see any witnesses in this room?"

"I want to talk to my lawyer!"

"This is a national security case. You don't get a damn lawyer! This is all about you giving us information that we deem vital to our national security interests. That's it, plain and simple."

The agent gave Gibson a couple of seconds to let it sink in. Then he went at him again.

"You know what my trump card is, Ronnie?"

The banker knew enough to keep his mouth shut and not answer the rhetorical question. "I can charge you with aiding and abetting terrorists by your cooperation with the drug cartel of your friend, Thomas Vasquez. Have your ass sent to Guantanamo," Herzog threatened.

"Then when you get there, we can put you in the cell with terrorists from the Middle East. We'll tell them you were a guard at Abu Ghraib Prison," Trupp added.

The FBI agents didn't say a word, they stared through him. The banker's bid for a sympathy play from anyone in the room was ignored. All he got in return was their icy, cold, glare.

Gibson was in so far over his head that he didn't know where to start. With both Harper and Dreyer gone he couldn't implicate anyone else. He felt slightly ill and was lightheaded. The sinking realization was that his name, not Harper's, was on every incriminating document. The obvious play was to give up Thomas Vasquez.

"So what's it going to be, a beating and a plane ride to Cuba? Or a chance to be able to walk on the Siesta Key beach some day?" Herzog snorted.

"What are we talking here in terms of jail time?" Gibson said as he tried to swallow.

"Depends on what you deliver and how fast," Herzog said.

"Where do you want to begin?" Gibson asked.

"Start this morning with Dreyer, and tell us everything this time."

"David left the bank between eight-thirty and nine. No sooner had he left than I got a call from Thomas. He wanted to know if David was here. I told him he had just taken off. He was really upset. He wouldn't tell me why he wanted to see him, but told me he had to see him right away. Then he slammed the phone down in my ear."

"What happened next?" Herzog asked.

"I called Thomas' condo. His wife Elena told me he got a phone call earlier in the day. The first call upset him. Then he made a call and flew out the door."

"Give us his phone number and the directions to his house," Herzog demanded.

Gibson handed him a card from his Rolodex file and wrote down directions to his condominium.

"We'll run over and check out his place. I doubt if he'll be there, but it's worth a shot. Maybe we can shake up his wife. You didn't happen to get a search warrant for his residence before you came down here, did you?" Tullis asked the Justice agent.

"We certainly did and one for Martin Harper's house, plane and boat, provided he owns a boat." Herzog reached inside his jacket and handed the FBI agent the search warrant.

"Martin owns a boat and so does Vasquez. They keep their boats at Siesta Key Marina. Vasquez owns a forty-three foot Donzi," Gibson chimed in.

"Glad you're cooperating. You may not go to Cuba after all," Tullis mocked the banker. The FBI agents headed for Vasquez' place.

"Rich, I'll call the Florida Highway Patrol and have them run Harper's and Vasquez' plates and put a statewide all-points bulletin on both cars. The FBI already has them out on Dreyer and his wife. Maybe one of the locals will spot one of them," Trupp offered.

"Don't forget to tell them we have a fugitive warrant on Vasquez."

"I'll make the call from Dreyer's office."

"You said that this morning was the last time you had any contact with Dreyer," Herzog continued.

"Yeah, I'm telling the truth. I tried to reach him on his cell phone a little while later, but the call wouldn't go through."

"What about Harper?"

"He's out of the country, down in the islands."

Guzman walked into the room with Gibson's secretary, who was carrying a box of computer printouts and a box of discs. "We're still going through the information, but I found a bunch of transfers for over ten thousand dollars, enough information to make a conspiracy charge stick."

He set the records down in the middle of Gibson's desk and started to walk back out of the office. Herzog stepped over to him and whispered something in his ear and he shook his head. Guzman followed the secretary back into the computer room.

"Save me some time and tell me where everything is," Herzog told Gibson, pointing at the stack of printouts and discs.

"Most of the stuff you need is there," Gibson confirmed. "EFTs – you know, electronic funds transfers to different banks around the world, deposit records."

"Tell me how the whole operation worked, including the money laundering and secret bank accounts. Choose your words very carefully, beginning with the secret accounts and the flow of cash in and out of the bank." The agent stood up and gazed out the window behind Gibson's desk.

"Now before you start I want you to turn around and check out your Porsche. The tow truck operator is about to take your car to the federal impounding lot in Tampa."

"Why are you doing that?" Gibson shouted, as he whirled around and shuddered at what he saw through the window.

"Agent Guzman took the liberty of calling the tow truck operator from your assistant's office twenty minutes ago. He suspects your car was used to transport cocaine."

"That's crazy. I never did that," the banker countered.

Herzog went over to Gibson, stood behind him, and put his hands on his shoulder.

"I'd be willing to bet we could find trace levels of cocaine inside if we had to. Now isn't the time to hold back on me Ronnie. You're really trying my patience."

"OK, OK, enough! I have the codes for the secret accounts in my computer. The keys to the kingdom. Everything is there."

"See, that wasn't so hard."

Herzog motioned to Guzman and the tow truck operator let the front end of the car slam to the ground from a height of four feet.

Gibson jumped up, shrieking at Herzog, "What the hell did you do that for?"

"Because you needed some motivation. I was wrong about you being slow on the uptake. You aren't slow. You're just damned uncooperative."

"How can you say that?" he pleaded

"Because you've been jerking me around ever since I set foot in the door. Are we on the same page now?" the agent blared.

"Yeah! OK," the banker said as he slithered down in his chair, resigned to his fate.

"Thomas would have money shipped up from Miami every week to ten days and we would park it here before shipping it out. There were times when we had so damn much cash we had to physically ship it around to other branches in town before sending it off to Switzerland."

"How did you ship it to Switzerland?" the investigator asked.

"In diplomatic pouches and suitcases with Martin Harper. He went to Switzerland at least twice a month, and down to the Caymans. With the amount of money we had coming in we physically couldn't keep it all here at this branch. Shipping it out and getting it laundered over in Europe was the only answer. That's why Martin flew over there so much."

"Where else does the money trail go?"

"Liechtenstein, the Caymans, Antigua and Panama. We have offshore accounts in all those countries for Thomas and for us. By the time the money recirculated back into his accounts it had gone through a half dozen foreign accounts and shell companies. Oh, I forgot about Tortola. Martin is flying back from setting up that location as we speak."

The muscles in Herzog's jaws flexed. "Where is he flying into?"

"The airport here in Sarasota," Gibson answered as if it were an off-hand remark.

Trupp walked back into the room, picking up the last bit of the conversation. "Do you want me to go over there and pick him up?"

"Yeah, get over there as quick as you can and take Guzman with you. Call ahead and have Sarasota PD assist. Chances are they can be there sooner than you guys can. "

"Right. Can you handle what's going down at the bank without our help?"

"Yeah, I'm going to be here awhile. Do me a favor and have Guzman bring Gibson's assistant and all the information she has back here to his office on your way out."

"I'll call you from the airport," Trupp said.

Herzog stepped around Gibson's desk, slid a chair over and sat down next to him as his secretary entered the office. He focused on the computer screen. Herzog told the secretary, "Bring up the spreadsheets for Vasquez' accounts first. I want you to pull out all the electronic fund transfers from Caribbean Ventures and from the shell company which is called...." he prompted.

"Gulf Coast Properties," Gibson blurted out.

"Brenda, pull up those two companies and separate them from all of the rest of the transfers," the agent instructed.

"Yes sir."

The assistant pressed the button and the printer began shooting out paper. Herzog's cell phone rang. Tullis was on the other end of the line.

Herzog listened for a couple of seconds and remarked, "That's not a surprise. I didn't figure Vasquez would be there. Did you get anything from his wife?"

"No. She was tough to read. She's either out of the loop or really cagey. I did get some papers out of his safe, but nothing that looks too promising," Tullis told him.

"Are you going to bring her in?" Herzog persisted.

"Yeah, we have Sarasota PD taking her in and a couple of uniforms sitting on the condo in case Vasquez tries to come back or make contact."

"Gibson told me that Vasquez and Harper have slips at Siesta Key Marina. Why don't you guys check that out and get back to me," Herzog told the FBI agent.

"Ed and I can be there in five minutes. We passed the harbor on the way over," Tullis told him.

"We may be able to round up one missing piece to the puzzle. Harper's flying into Sarasota and

I sent Trupp and Guzman over to the airport to pick him up."

"We'll let you know what's shaking down at the marina," Tullis said.

"Vasquez is still out there too, you and Ed be careful," Herzog told the FBI agent.

Chapter Fifty-One

SARASOTA AIRPORT – 3:30 PM

Kevin pulled back on the yoke and the Gulfstream began rolling down the runway. Their turn around in Sarasota had taken less than an hour. Just long enough to file a new flight plan and have Paul get some food for them. The only debate was whether to gas up there or in Ft. Myers. The latter won out. They decided to get going, because they didn't want Harper to beat them down there.

After they got out over Sarasota Bay, he banked the plane to the south and headed along the coastline. He had Paul call back to the tower. When he did, the chief of operations patched through a call. Paul took control of the aircraft and Kevin spoke on his headset.

"This is special agent Trupp with the Department of Justice. Who am I speaking with?" the voice on the other end said.

"Captain Kevin Henry, aircraft TANGO 109983."

"Is this Martin Harper's plane?"

"Yes sir, the corporate jet for Gulfcoast Bank," he vouched.

"What is your position?"

"We're approximately fifty miles north of Ft. Myers. Our ETA is fifteen minutes."

"Is Martin Harper on board?" Kevin got a sick feeling in the pit of his stomach.

"No sir, he's not. He got off in Sarasota."

"That slippery bastard!" Trupp vented.

The pilot got a weird look on his face. "Excuse me?"

"Sorry, I have a warrant for his arrest and need to know where he is," the Justice agent told him.

"He got off the plane when we landed an hour ago. He's supposed to meet us down in Ft. Myers. Mr. Harper told me that we would pick up his wife Judith and then fly down to the Keys," the pilot said.

The agent told the pilot to hold on while he talked the matter over with Guzman. When he came back on the line he said, "After you land the aircraft stay on board, and make no attempt to take off. I repeat, make no attempt to take off for Key West. I'll have authorities on the ground meet you. Do not leave the plane for any reason. Do you understand?"

"Yes sir. I'll await your instructions," Henry said as a sense of relief washed over him.

Trupp pressed a button on his cell phone and ended the conversation. He went back to his car with Guzman and called Herzog.

"Harper slipped past us. He landed an hour ago and had his corporate jet take off for Ft. Myers without him. I was able to get a hold of the pilot. He told me that Harper is supposed to meet his wife down in Ft. Myers. Then the game plan was to fly on to Key West," a dejected Trupp grumbled.

"So what's the status with the plane?" Herzog asked.

"After I got the information from the pilot I told him to keep it on the ground, in case Harper beats us there. Our issue is time. It'll take at least an hour for us to get to Ft. Myer's airport. Harper has a head start. Can you get an FBI or Coast Guard helicopter down there before we arrive?" Trupp asked.

"I don't know if there are any Coast Guard units stationed around here. I think everything is up in Tampa, but I'll ask Tullis and get back to you. Sit tight for a couple of minutes," Herzog said.

Chapter Fifty-Two

GULFCOAST BANK – 3:30 PM

Before Herzog could reach Tullis his cell phone rang.

"Mark, I was just about to call you," Herzog said.

"Well, the news here isn't good," the FBI agent informed him.

"What's going on?"

"The guy who runs the marina told us that Vasquez' boat left his slip about two hours ago. He's well out in the open waters of the Gulf by now in a forty-three foot Donzi. The way that thing hauls ass Vasquez can be in the Keys or the Bahamas in a couple of hours."

"Damn, we struck out again. But maybe all's not lost," Herzog reflected.

"What do you mean?" Tullis said.

"The reason I was going to call you was to see if we could get a chopper from either your department or the Coast Guard to go after Harper. Turns out we have two fugitives on the run, Harper and Vasquez."

"The answer to your question is yes. We can get a chopper here and in Tampa. How do you want to handle it?" Tullis asked.

"We missed Harper, and grabbing him is the first priority. Long story short is that his plane landed, he got off and the plane went on down to Ft. Myers. He's probably headed there by car as we speak. My concern is that Trupp and Guzman won't get down there soon enough. He'll have a plane sitting on the ground waiting when he arrives. Trupp talked to the pilot and he's not going anywhere, but I don't want Harper to slip the net because he gets spooked."

"We got some options, Rich. There's a Coast Guard unit stationed at Sarasota Airport. Have your guy go to their hangar at the west end of the airport. The Coast Guard can take them down to Ft. Myers. That solves the first problem," Tullis told Herzog.

"I'll buzz Trupp and they can be on their way. But how do we go after Vasquez?" Herzog questioned.

"I'll see if they can deploy a second chopper so we can chase down Vasquez. Ed and I will go after them with the second unit if it's available. If not, we can get a FBI bird out of Tampa. I also think we should involve Miami Coast Guard and use both air and sea interdiction."

"I agree Mark. Can you call and make the arrangements?"

"Affirmative. We're headed over to the airport right now. I'll touch base when I confirm what help the Coast Guard can give us."

"Sounds good," the Justice agent said, relieved that Tullis had stepped up to the plate for him.

Herzog hung up the phone and turned on Gibson. "Ronnie, help me out with something. Why would Harper get off the plane here in Sarasota after he landed and then drive down to Ft. Myers to catch a hop to Key West?"

He punched in Trupp's number and waited for Gibson's answer.

The banker became fidgety, rubbing his hands together and tugging on his tie. He opened his mouth to speak, but Herzog cut him off before he got started with a slicing motion across his throat.

"Russ, there's a Coast Guard squadron stationed at the airport. Tullis is making arrangements for you guys to take a bird down to Ft. Myers. Where are you now?"

"We're sitting in the terminal parking lot," the detective confirmed.

"Good, they're at the west end of the airport. Have airport security escort you out there. The FBI agents are on their way to take a second bird to go after Vasquez. He left the marina a while ago. You have first priority though. Get in the air as soon as you can. I'm staying put. Give me a shout when you get there."

"Will do, Rich."

Herzog sat his phone on the desk and motioned with his hand for Gibson to proceed.

"The only thing I can figure is that he got spooked," Gibson sputtered.

"What the hell are you talking about? Why would he get spooked?" Herzog snapped. "Why would he file a flight plan for the Keys out of Ft. Myers? Why not just turn around and go out of here? Why even stop? When is the last time you spoke with him?"

"I was on the phone with him when you busted in the front door," the banker said sheepishly.

"Why didn't you tell me that an hour ago?" Herzog bristled.

"Because you didn't ask?"

Herzog slammed his fist on the desk, stood up, and grabbed the banker with a hand full of shirt. "You just kissed your car goodbye you worthless son-of-a-bitch."

Herzog's cell phone rang and he let the banker go.

Tullis was on the other end. "Sarasota PD just found Dreyer's Lexus. It was torched in an abandoned farm house on the outskirts of Sarasota County. There was a body in the trunk. We have to assume that it's Dreyer, but identification will have to be confirmed through dental records to verify it's him."

"Dammit! How did Vasquez know he was meeting you guys?"

"Short of a phone tap or bug, I don't know, unless they got to his wife. Hopefully she's out there somewhere. Maybe she'll surface. In the meantime we'll keep monitoring Vasquez' cell phone and his land line. If he calls maybe we can triangulate his location through his cell phone," Tullis said as his voice trailed off.

"Appreciate the update."

Herzog glared at Gibson after the call ended. The banker looked away as a sinking feeling overwhelmed him.

"What? Did your guys find David? Is he OK?"

"No, you dirt bag, he's not OK." Herzog leaned across the desk, his face six inches from Gibson. "Vasquez killed him. Burned his car with him inside, and his wife is missing too. Is there anything you forgot to tell me?"

Gibson pushed his chair back and felt the blood rush from his face. "Yeah, there is one thing I forgot about. Martin had me transfer a million in cash over to the branch near his house on University Parkway this afternoon," he admitted.

"You son-of-a-bitch!"

Herzog threw a scratch pad of paper at him. "Give me directions to his house and the bank." Herzog called Sarasota PD.

Chapter Fifty-Three

SARASOTA – 5:00 PM

When Herzog reached the Gulfcoast bank branch on University Parkway there were two cars sitting in front of the bank. Harper's wasn't one of them. Both belonged to the Sarasota PD. He rolled down the window, flashed his badge and asked the patrolmen to stick around. He gave them his cell phone number in case Harper showed up.

Herzog rang Trupp back to see if they were on their way to Ft. Myers. No luck. So he left Trupp a message on his voice mail. Thirty seconds later he got a call back.

"Rich, can you hear me? It's Russ, returning your call."

"I hear you loud and clear. Are you in the air?"

"We are. We should be on the ground in Ft. Myers in about twenty minutes. Tullis radioed to our chopper from his that the Coast Guard got a GPS signal south of Naples. They won't have a visual for awhile but they think it's Vasquez' boat."

"Did Tullis lift off right after you?" Herzog asked.

"He did, a couple of minutes later. He said to tell you he had a Coast Guard cutter and a high-speed chase boat heading north out of Marathon to intercept the boat. They haven't been able to establish any radio contact with the craft in question. Given their speed, and the fact that they won't respond over the radio, it pretty much confirms it's Vasquez," Trupp told him.

"Did Tullis fill you in about Dreyer?"

"Yeah, maybe the banditos will resist and they can blow their sorry asses out of the water."

"They're toast if they resist. The Coast Guard doesn't screw around. If they hail a boat and no one responds their SOP is to lay a barrage from a fifty caliber machine gun over their bow. If the Vasquez boat returns fire or continues to run, then the Coast Guard has standing orders to disable it by whatever means necessary," Herzog affirmed.

"That makes my day. I hope they do something stupid so the Coast Guard can grease them."

"Would that be great or what? I'm heading over to Harper's house. Stay in touch Russ."

"I'll bring you up to speed after we land in Ft. Myers."

Chapter Fifty-Four

COAST GUARD CHOPPER ZEBRA 185 - 5:00 PM

"Agent Tullis, this is Coast Guard Commander Robinson. Our cutter intercepted the boat in question south of Largo."

"Did they resist?" Tullis yelled as he tried to overcome the whirl of the helicopter blades outside the cabin.

"Affirmative sir. They tried to evade capture and ignored several warning volleys. My crew disabled the craft and picked up the survivors."

"Where are you taking them?" Tullis asked.

"To our dock in Marathon. You can meet us there and question the survivors."

"Did they have any identification?"

"No sir. Neither of them had any identification on them and they're not talking."

"Appreciate the update, Commander."

The two FBI agents took off their head sets and leaned towards one another.

"I'm betting that Vasquez wasn't on board. He probably sent his two flunkies out as a decoy. What do you think?" Honner said.

"You're probably right, Ed. Why take a boat when you got a plane? If Vasquez isn't one of the guys they picked up he may still be hanging around Sarasota. I better call Herzog and give him a heads-up."

The pilot handed the FBI agent a satellite phone and he rang Herzog.

"Rich, this is Tullis. The Coast Guard apprehended Vasquez' boat near Largo, but there were only two people on board. We don't know their identity yet, but we're meeting them in Marathon. We have photos of Vasquez, Estacio and Batista. Although neither of the men in custody is talking, my gut instinct is that Vasquez isn't one of them."

"Thanks for the update. I'm headed to Harper's house," Herzog said.

"We'll call back when we know more," Tullis promised.

Herzog rolled up to the security gate at University Park Estates and waited for the guard to come out of his house. The entry gate was down and the guard was sitting behind a closed glass door talking on the telephone.

"Come on, come on," Herzog complained. He hit the horn a couple of times before the security guard, a grey haired man in a dark green sport coat, got out of his seat and put the phone down. Herzog flashed his badge and the disgruntled guard opened the glass door. "Has Mr. Harper come through the gate since you came on duty?"

"Yes sir, within the past half hour."

"How do I get to Nantucket Lane?" he snarled.

"It's off the main road, the one you are on. About a mile and a half back. Go past the golf course and tennis courts, then take a right onto Stowe and then another right on Nantucket. If you go past the lake, you've gone too far. But you shouldn't have any problem finding it."

"Here's my card and cell number. If you see Mr. Harper come to the gate call me immediately."

The guard nodded and pressed the button, the bar swung up. Herzog blew by it and spotted his first landmark, the golf club entrance, off to the right. He passed the tennis courts and kept driving until he saw the sign for Stowe Court. The agent waited for a couple of bikers to clear the jogging trail that ran across the front of the street, then hung a right on Stowe. When he got on Nantucket, he slowed to a crawl and stopped when he saw Harper's address.

The house was a salmon colored, Mediterranean style villa in the middle of a cul-de-sac. He turned off the ignition and strained to see any movement inside the spacious, dimly lit house. After he got a glimpse of Harper, Herzog changed his phone from ring to vibrate mode. As soon as he opened the car door to get out he felt the vibration of his cell phone. He pulled the door back and pressed the talk button.

"Agent Herzog, this is the Tampa FBI office. We've received a tip a few minutes ago that Thomas Vasquez was going to be at Siesta Key Marina. We contacted Sarasota PD and they're sending a swat team in. Agent Tullis advised us that's what we needed to do. Do you want to participate in the operation?"

"No, I'm not able to, but keep me advised of the situation," Herzog instructed.

"Yes sir."

He sat there for a moment trying to decipher what he had been told. Who would have given the Bureau this new tip, and how reliable was it?

Herzog couldn't devote any more time trying to figure the relevance of the latest piece of information. He turned off the phone, slipped it inside his jacket and slid out of the car. The agent nudged the door shut with his shoulder to minimize the sound. He crept up to the right side of the house with his weapon drawn. He could see that the front door was cracked open a hair. Herzog ducked behind the cover of a banyan tree twenty feet to the right of the door.

Chapter Fifty-Five

MARATHON, FLORIDA – 5:30 PM

When the swish of the helicopter blades stopped, the two FBI agents hopped down onto the wood plank pier, about fifty yards from the Coast Guard cutter. They were met by the ship's commander.

"I'm Commander Robinson."

The agents introduced themselves and shook hands with him. "You and your crew did a great job running these guys down. You apprehended a pair of real bad asses. Where are they being held? We need to identify them ASAP," Tullis said.

"Right this way sir. Follow me."

The officer led them to a maintenance hangar. Two of his crewmen were pointing their M-16's at a couple of guys sitting on a concrete floor, sharing a soaking wet olive drab blanket. The fugitives had their hands tied behind their backs with plastic wrist restraints. Both looked over as the agents walked into the building. The two muttered to one another in rapid-fire Spanish, but stopped when the agents got close to them.

Honner took a hard look at them. His shoulders dropped and his arms fell to his sides. Tullis ran his hand through his hair and scratched his head. He took a step away and kicked the air with his foot.

Then just as quickly he whirled around and knelt down in front of them. "Where's your boss, Thomas Vasquez?" he yelled at them. *"Donde esta tu jefe?"*

Neither man was intimidated. The smaller of the two, Estacio, cowered but didn't speak.

Tullis tried another tactic to make his point. *"No habla Ingles?"* Estacio gave his partner a harried look but neither spoke.

"Well I know you'll *habla* this: We know who you are, senor Batista, senor Estacio. You guys are going away for twenty years just on the drug trafficking counts," Tullis said with a smile. "The news just keeps getting worse. That Lexus that you two dirt bags torched earlier today with the body stuffed into the trunk! We found that, too."

Neither man budged, but Tullis continued hammering away. "I need your clothes. After these guards untie you, take them off and toss them over to me. I'm sure that forensics can match the residue on your pants and shirts with soil samples we recovered from the crime scene. I don't want to have a problem attaching murder charges to your drug trafficking charges."

Tullis jumped up and rubbed his hands back and forth then boasted, "Florida is a death penalty state, and what you fools did today buys you a ticket to the dance. I doubt that your boss told you that when you were torching Dreyer's car with him inside," the agent snapped at them.

The guards cut their wrist bands, and the two men looked at each before starting to take their clothes off. Estacio gestured with his hands and fired off a burst of Spanish to his partner.

One of the enlisted men spoke up, translating. "I don't know if you heard all that, but the guy who started the conversation wants to give up his boss. The other one threatened to kill him if he opens his mouth to you."

The FBI agent stomped over to Batista, threw an elbow to his chest and knocked him to the floor in one quick move. Honner drew his weapon and pointed it at Batista's head while Tullis yanked the Colombian's arms behind his back and put a new restraint around his wrists. The agent jerked him to his feet and pulled the naked prisoner away by his hair. When he was about thirty feet away from Estacio he pulled out his weapon and placed it against his temple. "Tell me how you guys killed Dreyer today, and where Vasquez is!" Tullis demanded.

"Go screw yourself."

"OK big man, we'll see who's screwed! Commander, rev up the chopper," he shouted to the pilot. "We need to go out over the bay. I have to drop this guy off in a secret location. Ed, give me a hand with this shithead. After we get him on board, work on Estacio."

The two men grabbed Batista under the arms and dragged him over to helicopter. He screamed out something, but the roar of the blades hid whatever he was ranting about. The prisoner wretched and contorted trying to resist being put inside the helicopter. Then he stopped moving entirely and slumped to the ground. The two agents had enough. They heaved his body in the passenger compartment of the helicopter. He hit with a thud on the metal grated floor and was still thrashing around and cursing as Tullis closed the door. The agent gave instructions to the pilot, and the aircraft took off from the pier, disappearing over the Gulf.

After they were in the air about five minutes Tullis slid the door back and reached for the Colombian. Batista kicked at him. Tullis clubbed him in the kidneys with his fists a couple of times before he dragged him by the scruff of the neck to the edge of the door. He dangled his feet out of the chopper. Batista pulled back as he tried to resist being tossed out.

"Pay attention dirt bag. We're five miles out over shark-filled water. That cut on your leg is like a dinner bell to them. Once you're in the water I give you five, maybe ten minutes, before you're chum. But just to give you a chance, one that you never gave the guy you killed today, I'll untie your wrist bracelets and give you a life jacket. That way you can try and swim to shore, or if you don't know how to swim you can flail around in the water and attract more sharks," Tullis said in a menacing tone.

"If I dropped you out of the chopper at this altitude with your hands tied and no vest, you would just sink to the bottom like a cannon ball. Die in a couple of minutes by drowning. No justice in that, much too quick. At least this way I get to sit fifty feet above the water and watch some man eating machine rip you limb from limb!"

"No, no! Don't toss me out. I'll tell you whatever you want to know."

Tullis pulled Batista back by his wrists just far enough so that his feet were still dangling out of the open door. He put his gun to the base of his spine and pulled the hammer back on his Glock 40.

"Where's Vasquez?"

"After he killed the banker, we dumped the car at the farm house and went to the marina. He told us to take the boat to Bimini. That he would fly down later tonight. Said he had unfinished business in Sarasota."

"What did that mean to you?" Tullis asked

"That he couldn't trust the guys at the bank anymore."

"You mean that he was going to get rid of them like he did Dreyer?" Tullis asked.

"Yeah."

"I'm going to cut the plastic tie around your wrists. If you make any attempt to move, I'll shoot you and kick your ass out the door."

Batista got the message. He sat motionless with his feet dangling outside the helicopter. Tullis put a metal handcuff above the plastic tie, and attached the other end of the handcuff to the door handle. Then he slid it back forcing Batista to move with it.

Tullis asked the pilot for the satellite phone. He called Herzog but missed him. So he left a message on his voice mail. He told him that Vasquez was still in the area, probably going after Gibson and Harper.

He called Tampa to find out what was happening. His assistant, Karey, took the call. She told him that Vasquez hadn't shown up at the marina, and Harper hadn't shown up in Ft. Myers.

Tullis paused for a while and tried to get his head around everything.

He told his assistant, "I thought it was long shot that we could pinch Vasquez at the marina. The only other person who would know what's going on is Harper. Vasquez would be too smart to go back to the marina," he added.

"We're going to fly back to Sarasota and question these guys along the way. I'll know how everything is tied together by the time we land," the agent declared.

"If I hear anything from Agents Trupp or Herzog I'll call you immediately."

"Thanks, Karey."

The helicopter headed back to the dock at Marathon. Tullis sat down next to the prisoner. "Now tell me all about the murder of Senator Harrington, and remember —you can still end up in the drink if I think you're holding out on me."

Chapter Fifty-Six

MARTIN HARPER'S HOUSE- 5:30 PM

Herzog crept along the edge of the curved driveway with his nine millimeter pointed at the door. When he reached the portico, he took one quick step up and kicked the partially open door back against the wall. He stepped inside the house and drew a bead on Harper with his weapon. He told him not to move.

The banker was standing at the opposite end of the thirty foot marble entryway, his face pale and gray. He stood there, frozen in place, an oversized suitcase in each hand. Herzog motioned with the gun for him to put the luggage down. Harper didn't respond. The agent closed the door with his foot and walked towards him.

"Put the suitcases down," the agent ordered.

Harper snapped out of it and set the luggage down on the carpet just inside the entrance to the dining room. The banker stared at him through foggy eyes.

"I'm not here to kill you, just to arrest you Mr. Harper. I'm Special Agent Herzog from the

Department of Justice. You're under arrest for money laundering and racketeering."

"Can I sit down? I don't feel so good," Harper muttered.

"Yeah, after I pat you down. Turn around, spread eagle. Put your palms against the wall."

Like a man in slow motion, Harper followed the orders. The agent walked over to him and frisked him with his free hand. Satisfied that he wasn't a threat he told him, "Go ahead and sit down."

Harper sauntered a couple of steps into the great room to his left and eased down on a yellow, floral print sofa. Herzog followed him and paused at the entrance to the room. He put his nine millimeter back in the holster.

"The FBI is over at your bank poring over documents. Gibson has already given me the records on Caribbean Ventures, your shell company, the electronic funds transfers and all the offshore account information."

The banker was unfazed by what Herzog had just told him, a blank stare was all that registered. Herzog jolted him by saying, "Your partner Vasquez killed your son-in-law today. We recovered his body from the trunk of his burned-out car in the middle of an orange grove."

Harper grimaced and looked back at Herzog. "That miserable bastard. I can't believe he did that. What about my daughter Sarah?" he uttered with his eyes glazing over.

"We haven't been able to find her. I don't know what happened to her." Herzog's voice grew louder. "Mr. Harper, you were in bed with a real piece of work. Now your son-in-law is dead, and who knows what happened to your daughter. All because of you and Gibson. You guys are going to be cell mates for a long time. The only way you can hope to make it right is by giving up Vasquez. If you help me get him,

I might be able to guarantee that you don't die an old man in prison. But I have to know right now. Where can I find him?"

Harper's head sunk down to his chest, and his hands began to tremble. He stared down at the floor and murmured back like a man in a confessional. "He has a house in Key Biscayne and a Cessna Citation at Palm Beach Airport, in case you didn't know. And I assume you know that he has a condo over at the Palm Island Club and a Donzi here in Sarasota."

"Don't move." Herzog reached over to the phone sitting on the glass and steel coffee table in front of Harper. He dialed the number for the FBI office in Tampa. "I need to talk to Agent Tullis," he said, "Can you patch me through?"

"Yes sir," the voice on the other end told him.

Tullis was on the line in seconds. "Mark, this is Rich. I got Harper. He told me that Vasquez has a Cessna Citation at Palm Beach Airport and a house on Key Biscayne."

"We'll check both of them out, but I don't think he's down here yet. We picked up two of his guys, and one of them told me Vasquez had unfinished business in Sarasota."

"What's that mean?"

"His guy thought he was going to take care of business with Harper and Gibson before he took off. That he was going to take them out, like he did Dreyer. Where are you now?"

"I'm at Harper's house."

"Oh shit! Get the hell out of there! Grab Harper and get out of there now! You already got Gibson, so he's the next target."

"Thanks for the warning, Mark. I'll hook up with you later."

Herzog hung the phone up and yelled at Harper. "Leave everything. We have to get out of here. Vasquez is looking for you!"

Chapter Fifty-Seven

MARTIN HARPER'S HOUSE – 5:45 PM

The front door flew open. Herzog and Harper spun around at the same time. They saw the silhouette of Thomas Vasquez in the doorway brandishing a Mac 10 submachine gun. The agent reached for his nine millimeter, but he wasn't fast enough. Vasquez gestured with his weapon and shook his head from side to side, "No, no, no!"

Herzog slowly pulled his hand away. His eyes blazing, the Colombian kicked the door closed and inched towards them. He stopped ten feet away on the other side of the hallway.

"Martin, Martin, I can't believe all the trouble you and David have caused me. All you had to do was take care of your son-in-law. You and Harrington were exactly alike. Neither of you carried out your end of the bargain," he said. Like a father scolding a disobedient child.

Harper didn't respond.

"And who is this — the FBI agent your son-in-law called this morning?"

Harper looked back at him, unnerved by the question. "No, ah...he's the chauffeur I called to take me to the airport," the banker responded.

"Really? I didn't know the limousine services used Fords," the Colombian derided him.

Vasquez looked over at the agent and told him, "Take your gun and wallet out of your jacket with your left hand. Use two fingers. Then place them at your feet. Put your hands on your head, and slide the gun and your wallet over to me with your foot."

Herzog placed the gun at his feet, then took his wallet out of his jacket and slid it across to Vasquez, all the while keeping his hands behind his head.

"Department of Justice," Vasquez read from the open wallet.

The agent looked back at him but didn't speak.

"Slide your gun over to me with your foot, very slowly."

Herzog glared back and hesitated for a couple of seconds.

"Do it now," Vasquez commanded, as he trained the weapon on the agent.

He kicked the gun hard across the marble floor. When Vasquez squatted down to pick it up, Harper bolted. Vasquez turned and unleashed a burst of fire from the Mac 10. A couple of bullets ricocheted off the plaster wall before cutting Harper down as he tried to make it around the corner and into the kitchen. He fell over a chair, landing face down on the floor between the granite counter top and the kitchen table.

Herzog took two quick steps and sprang at Vasquez' mid section, knocking him against the wall. They tumbled down to the marble floor. The agent tried to wrestle the machine gun out of his hand while both men rolled back and forth on the floor.

The agent rolled away from the barrel just before Vasquez squeezed off a burst. Bullets whizzed by his ear and sprayed the wall across from them. The percussion stunned him briefly, but he maintained his grip on the barrel of the gun. Herzog squirmed on top of Vasquez, and pushed as hard as he could with his left arm to force the barrel of the gun down. Then he slammed Vasquez in the jaw with his right elbow. This broke the Colombian's grip.

The force it took to separate Vasquez from the weapon rolled Herzog over on his side with his back to Vasquez. He turned as fast as he could and pressed the trigger. It was jammed. The Mac 10 didn't fire.

Vasquez dove for Herzog's nine millimeter lying on the marble floor a few feet away. Herzog kicked at his weapon but couldn't quite reach it. He slid the breach back on the Mac 10 and pressed the trigger again. Nothing…

Vasquez grabbed the nine millimeter and squeezed off three rounds as Herzog tried to roll away from the flash of the gun. Two of them hit their mark. Herzog's leg and shoulder felt the searing pain as the bullets burned into them. A third round grazed the side of his head and went into the wall next to him. Herzog dropped the Mac 10 and rolled over on his back, unable to move. Blood gushed from his leg. The hallway took on a hazy cast as he tried to focus on the shadowy figure across the room from him.

Herzog's brain told him to reach for the gun next to him, but his arm wouldn't move. He squinted but could only make out Vasquez's lower torso.

The killer pointed the hand gun at Herzog as he lay there writhing in pain. "You did the right thing agent. I respect you for that. You knew I was going to kill you after I killed Martin. You have a sense of survival. Just like me. We probably have more in common than you think."

Summoning every ounce of strength he could, and knowing that he was about to finish him off, Herzog mumbled just loud enough for Vasquez to hear, "You're just another greaseball killer."

Two shots rang out and Herzog slipped into darkness.

Chapter Fifty-Eight

MARTIN HARPER'S HOUSE – 6:00 PM

Sarah Dreyer stopped at the archway and looked down at the body of her father immersed in a pool of blood. She knelt next to him, disregarding the sea of red that covered the floor. She laid her revolver on the floor and pressed her fingers to his carotid artery. Her shoulders slumped. She was too late.

She dabbed his forehead with her sleeve and tried in vain to wipe the blood away as her tears dropped on his face. Sarah laid her head on his blood soaked shirt and murmured, "Daddy, why? Why did it have to come to this?" she sobbed.

After a couple of minutes she got the strength to stand up. Her white capri pants were crimson from her knees down. She hovered over him, tears flowing freely.

Then Sarah moved over to the agent lying on his back. She reached down to pick up his wallet. When she saw the badge, she knelt down next to him and pressed the veins in his neck to see if he had a pulse. It was thready.

As she looked for some other sign of life from the agent, her eyes caught the empty stare on Thomas Vasquez' face, blood oozing from his mouth. She felt a cold anger.

Sarah lifted her head up from Herzog's chest and saw the wound in his shoulder. A small stream of blood was trickling down from his forehead. But it was the purple, syrupy pool by his leg that concerned her.

She knew what had to be done. Sarah scurried back into the kitchen and found a dish towel. She grabbed a serrated-edged knife from the granite counter.

Dropping to Herzog's side, she tore his pant leg open with the knife and pressed the towel down into the wound. His spongy flesh turned the towel a deep red. She struggled to remove the belt from his slacks. After she got it through the last belt loop she eased it under his thigh. Then she wrapped it around the wound and pulled it though the buckle until it was as tight as she could get it. Sarah pulled back on the loose end and tucked it underneath his leg. The flow of blood slowed and nearly stopped.

She hurried back to the great room, passing two yellow suitcases, picked up the phone and dialed the paramedics. "Hello 911! I have an emergency at 3410 Nantucket Lane in University Park Estates. There are three gunshot victims. One is still alive. You need to get over here right away."

"Ma'am, I am going to need you to stay on the line and give me more information."

"Lady, I don't have time to deal with you. Just get the damn EMT unit over here now," Sarah ranted.

She tossed the phone aside. Back in the hallway she leaned over the back of the couch, grabbed a yellow pillow and took it back to Herzog. She placed the pillow under his feet, elevated them on Vasquez' torso and headed for the kitchen again.

At the sink she grabbed a dishcloth from the drawer and ran it under cold water. She twisted the rag to wring out most of the water, then returned to the nightmare in the hallway and bent down beside the agent. Sarah opened his shirt and blotted the wound in his shoulder. Then she wiped the blood that had streamed down the side of his face as she cupped his head with her other hand.

"Please don't die," she sobbed. "Hang on. Help's on the way."

She brushed back his blood soaked hair and dabbed at the wound in his temple. Then she reached under his leg and released the pressure on his thigh for a couple of seconds before tightening it back up again.

"Please dear God, don't let him die," she begged.

Off in the distance she heard the wail of the sirens. Her head turned instinctively towards the windows in the front of the house. She was startled when the agent reached for her, like a hand from the grave. He squeezed her arm.

Sarah turned around and lowered her face and said softly, "Hold on for a little longer, help's on the way," then she stroked the top of his hand.

"You saved my life. Who are you?" Herzog whispered, his narrowed eyes fixed on her.

"I'm Sarah Dreyer. My husband is David. Do you know what happened to him?" she pleaded.

Herzog rolled his eyes away and closed them. He grimaced, praying that the pained expression on his face hadn't betrayed the truth. A couple of seconds later he mumbled, "Don't know."

The sound of the sirens grew more piercing and Herzog opened his eyes again. He motioned with his hand for her to get closer to him. Sarah laid her left ear next to his mouth so that she could hear him.

"Hide the suitcases before anybody else gets here."

"What's in them?"

"Your family's future… Let some good come from all of this. Please!" the agent gasped.

She drew back from the agent and his eyes closed once again. His head began to roll gently towards the floor. Sarah cushioned his head, then put her hands to her face and began to sob. She had the answer about her husband David.

Sarah lowered her head to Herzog's chest and listened. His heartbeat grew more faint. She was torn between staying with him and doing what he asked her to do. The beleaguered woman looked over at the suitcases for a moment, then trained her eyes on the body lying beneath her. She couldn't walk away until she lowered her head to his chest one more time. She was certain his life was slipping away.

Conflicted, and physically drained, she was barley able to rise up. She managed to make it over to the suitcases, before she stopped and looked back at the agent. She struggled with the weight of the suitcase, but got enough of a grip on the handle to pull it out of the room.

The sliding glass door to the pool and patio was open. Sarah rolled it across the sandstone pool deck to the screen door entrance to the lanai. She pressed the door handle, and banged the suitcase against the metal screen door forcing it open. She dragged it out into the yard, and slid it along the grass perimeter until she reached the maintenance door for the pool. It was located at the base of the rear retaining wall, shielded by a row of juniper bushes.

Sarah lifted the open lock from the hasp. She pushed the small wood door back with her knee and sat the suitcase down behind the filter. She placed a dark blue pool cover over it. Then she went back into the house, grabbed the other suitcase, and repeated the process. After she locked the door she came back through the lanai and into the hallway. The front of the house was an explosion of red and blue flashing lights.

A couple of seconds later there was a series of hard knocks at the front door. That was followed by two men in suits who kicked the door open. They pointed their weapons directly at her. She saw two emergency medical technicians behind them, outside on the doorstep.

"Move away from the body ma'am," the shorter man with reddish hair commanded.

"I'm Sarah Dreyer, I'm the one who called 911. This is my father's house, Martin Harper. Thomas Vasquez killed him."

"Ma'am, step away from the bodies," the agent shouted.

Sarah shuffled back a couple of steps from the agent. The two men with guns drawn moved toward her. One of them waved the paramedic inside.

"Please, help the agent. He's dying. He has severe blood loss and he's in shock. He has a wound to the femoral artery," Sarah told them.

"Are you a nurse?" one of the paramedics asked as he walked over to the agent.

"In another life," Sarah mused.

The two lawmen put their weapon away and the EMT's crouched down by the victim.

Chapter Fifty-Nine

MARTIN HARPER'S HOUSE- 6:15 P.M.

"Mrs. Dreyer, we're sorry for your loss. I'm Detective Trupp, and this is Agent Guzman," he told her as they showed her their identification.

"What exactly are you telling me?"

"We mean for the loss of your father," Trupp quickly asserted.

"What about my husband?"

Trupp hesitated a couple of seconds before he answered. "Mrs. Dreyer, can we go somewhere and sit down?"

He asked Guzman to stay with the paramedics while he talked with Sarah. Then he followed her into the living room. They sat down on the sofa. Sarah folded her hands together as if she were praying. The silence in the room was deafening as Trupp searched for the right words.

He leaned closer to her, paused and said in a strained voice, "Mrs. Dreyer, I'm sorry to tell you this. We recovered the body of your husband late this afternoon. He was shot by Thomas Vasquez."

"No! No! That can't be!" Dreyer's wife wailed, as tears streamed down her face. She sagged back on the couch. "David's dead and Thomas Vasquez killed him, too. Why?"

She began sobbing uncontrollably, cupping her hands around her nose and mouth. Trupp offered her his handkerchief and touched her arm with his hand.

"David told me that there were problems at the bank," she sobbed. "He told me a little, but I never thought it would come to this. I guess that's why he gave me a key to a safe deposit box. He called it our life insurance policy. I guess that was what he intended to give to you," she murmured.

Sarah sniffled a couple of times and dabbed at her cheeks and nose. She choked herself off and said to the investigator, "Thank you for telling me this in private. I really don't know where to begin. I don't know what to do first."

Reeling from David's murder she looked for solace from the only person who could grant it to her, the messenger of death at her side. "What am I going to say to my girls? They're going to be devastated."

Trupp felt helpless, immersed in her plight, unable to relieve her pain. He stumbled and offered her the only plausible solution, support from her family.

"Are there any family members who can help you out?"

"I don't know, I guess maybe my sister and her husband."

As Trupp debated what to say next Sarah stunned the agent when she asked, "When can I see my husband? When will his body be released?"

The investigator was blind sided. He told her, "I'll let you know as soon as the coroner completes his investigation."

Sarah continued, "I don't know how to tell the girls or my mom."

"Mrs. Dreyer, you're going to have to take it one step at a time. Do you want me to speak with your mother and inform her of your father's death?" the agent volunteered.

"Thank you, but that's something I'll have to deal with. My mother is visiting her sister in Fort Lauderdale, she'll be back tomorrow."

Trupp didn't want to dredge up the shooting, but he had no choice. "Mrs. Dreyer, can you take a minute? Tell me why you came over to your parent's house, and what happened after you arrived here tonight."

She nodded to him and said, "I didn't have anywhere else to go. I rode around all day after I got David's panic phone call. I decided this was the safest place to go. I thought my dad was still down in the islands. So I called the house and nobody picked up. But when I got here I saw his car in the garage and two others near the driveway. I recognized Thomas Vasquez' Mercedes but not the other one. And after David's call this morning, I was concerned about my father. So I took the revolver from the console, got out and snuck around to the side of the house. David told me it would be there, the revolver I mean." Sarah stopped and took a deep breath.

Guzman strolled into the room and sat down next to them. Trupp told her, "Go ahead. Take your time."

She continued, "I hadn't been able to get a hold of my father all day. I was shaking like a leaf as I went around the side of the house. When I got to the bay window, I looked in and saw daddy lying on the floor in a pool of blood."

She gazed at Trupp, her eyes red and teary.

"Go ahead, take it slow and tell me the rest," he said in a soothing voice.

"I just slumped to the ground and began crying. I was crying so hard I was afraid that whoever was inside was going to hear me."

Sarah wiped her eyes again, and Trupp bit at his lip.

"When I able to finally pull myself together, I got up and walked around to the pool area. I kicked my shoes off and opened the screen door as quietly as I could. I tiptoed into the house through the lanai and heard someone talking in the entry foyer."

"When I got a little closer I recognized the voice of Thomas Vasquez. He threatened to kill the agent. The same way he shot my father."

Trupp kept digging. "What happened next?"

"I took a couple of steps and peeked around the corner wall of the kitchen, Vasquez had his back to me. Then the agent said something back to him that I couldn't hear very well. Vasquez pointed the gun down at his head, and that's when I fired two shots. He slumped to the floor and didn't move. I ran over to my father and tried to get a pulse, but I knew it was too late," Sarah recounted.

Trupp sensed she needed a breather as he looked over and saw the anguish on her face. "Do you want to take a break? Can I get you a glass of water?"

"No thanks, I'm OK." Trupp seemed unconvinced but was glad she wanted to forge ahead.

"After that I went into the foyer and saw the wallet lying on the floor, between the agent and Vasquez. I flipped it open and went over to the agent to see if I could help him. After I got him stabilized I called 911, and you guys came."

The agents sat there absorbing everything she had told them. Sarah was relieved that she had been able to detail her account of the horrendous ordeal.

Trupp started to say something, thought better of it, and Guzman jumped in.

"Mrs. Dreyer, can you tell us where the gun is that you used to shoot Vasquez?"

"Oh, yeah, it's ah, on the floor next to ah, next to my dad," Sarah said in a stupor like voice.

"Can you show us where?" Trupp persisted gently.

Sarah took a second before she stood up and walked over to her father's body. She pointed down, looked away from her dad, and slipped out to the pool area to grab her tennis shoes. She came back inside and held them in her hands staring down at her father's body.

Trupp put a latex glove on his right hand. He lifted the gun from the floor using a pen inside the trigger housing, returned to the hallway and handed the gun to Guzman. He opened a plastic evidence bag and dropped the weapon inside.

"This is the revolver she used on Vasquez," he told Guzman.

"She ought to get a medal for getting rid of that piece of garbage," Guzman affirmed.

"You got that right. She's one incredibly brave lady. That's why I have no intention of having her hang around until the crew from the crime lab gets here to do a GSR test on her."

"Which lab is going to do the house?" Guzman asked.

"The FBI forensic team is on their way down from Tampa. They can process the crime scene and the Mac 10 for Vasquez prints. As far as Mrs. Dreyer's .38 goes, that's just a formality."

"Good call. Why drag this out any longer and punish her for doing the right thing?" the DEA agent offered.

"When they arrive we'll have them process her weapon first, and forward all of the information back to Charlie Brune's office at DOJ. The crime scene here is to be regarded as classified information."

"I doubt if Tullis' boss is going to be happy with that," Guzman said with a hint of sarcasm.

"He'll get over it," Trupp replied. "The FBI is going to get credit for apprehending Harrington's killer, Carlos Batista. We'll give them our forensic evidence from Washington to make their case. As far as this deal here tonight goes, the truth is never going to see the light of day in the media. It's going to go down as a home invasion with two victims, the owner and the perp. The two events are never going to be connected."

For the first time all day a smile came to Guzman's face. "I'm glad you said that, because we have unfinished business with Vasquez' partners. This is just the tip of the iceberg for us. I'm thinking Gibson and the two Colombians can give us the skinny about the entire Vasquez operation."

"Hmmm," Trupp mumbled. Surprised and pleased at the DEA agent's train of thought.

"The way I see it, as long as we keep Vasquez name out of the news and keep Batista's identity under wraps, nobody is going to know what happened to either of them. The down side to this scenario is that we'll have a very short window of opportunity to go after the drug cartel," the detective pointed out.

"Yeah, I agree about the time factor. We can delay the release of Vasquez' body to his wife until we finish the investigation. We have to bury the press in some bullshit story. The combination of the two should buy us a little more time. Provided of course that my boss, Charlie, is willing to go along with the plan," Trupp theorized.

"Talk to your boss when you get back to Washington. Run the idea by him for continuation of the task force we have now, and see what he says."

"We all have a lot invested. Why quit now?" Trupp pondered.

"Oh, before I forget, I talked to the coroner's office while you were interviewing Mrs. Dreyer. He's willing to release her husband's body tomorrow morning if you can present him with verifiable dental records."

"Not good," Trupp grunted. "I don't think she's up for that, not after all this." He gestured at the scene around them.

The detective stepped back into the living room next to Sarah. He scanned her face trying to see if she could stand one more hit.

"Mrs. Dreyer, there's something else we need to talk about."

She braced herself and nodded for him to continue.

"Agent Guzman spoke with the medical examiner a while ago. Your husband's body can be released tomorrow morning pending identification."

Sarah interrupted, "What do you mean? Why is there a problem with his identification?"

Trupp wanted to minimize the shock value and measured his words very carefully. "The condition of your husband's body is the issue. They shot him and burned the car. His body was discovered in the trunk."

"Oh my God! Was he dead before the fire?" she gasped in horror.

"The coroner was able to confirm that he was."

Trupp spoke softly. "Mrs. Dreyer, if it's all right with you, I'll go down to the morgue tomorrow morning and do the identification for you. There's no need for you to be exposed to any more suffering. But I have to have his dental records to do that."

Sarah's eyes twitched as she tried to control her emotions. "I should do this, not you."

"You don't want to see him this way. You want to remember him the way he looked when he left the house this morning. Put that image in your mind and keep it there," he urged.

"Tell me when I can get his dental records and I'll make this part of it go away for you," he pleaded.

One of the paramedics walked into the room and told the investigator, "We're going to take Agent Herzog to Sarasota Trauma Center. He's stable. He asked if he could speak with Mrs. Dreyer before we take him out."

Sarah stepped into the hallway. Guzman and Trupp stood back in the great room. Herzog was conscious, lying on a gurney with a couple of IV tubes running into his left arm and a respirator covering his nose and mouth. The paramedic lifted the respirator up and moved back a short distance. Herzog peered up at Sarah and reached for her with his free hand and motioned her to get closer. She put the side of her face close to his mouth. "Thank you," he whispered in her ear. "You saved my life. I can never repay you for what you did," he told her.

She pulled back just enough to gaze back into his eyes. She squeezed his hand and declared, "You already have. You're still alive."

Sarah gave him a tearful smile that only he could see. He answered with a tiny smile of his own, and Sarah released his hand. The EMT secured the respirator to his face before wheeling him toward the front door.

Trupp and Guzman walked out to Herzog and spoke to him for a couple of seconds. He gave them a thumbs up with his right hand, and the paramedics wheeled him out to the ambulance.

Sarah edged back to the kitchen area and stood next to her father's body as the paramedics lifted up the gurney. She touched his cheek with her palm and kissed his forehead

"The forensic team will be here shortly," Trupp told her. "The only area they have to look at is the interior of the house, and that won't take very long. So you shouldn't have any problems getting back inside the house tomorrow."

"I appreciate that. I know that I have to get things cleaned and straightened up before my mother gets back. I don't want anyone to see the house this way. Here is our dentist's phone number," she told him as she handed him an appointment card.

"I'll call the medical examiner and inform him that I'll be identifying the body for you. I'm glad you decided to let me do this for you," the detective said.

"I realized that what you said made a lot of sense. I just have a hard time with it. I feel like I'm shirking my responsibility."

"You're doing the right thing. I know at this time that it's not much consolation to you, but you did save a life today. You spared Agent Herzog's family from the pain you're going through. We all owe you a debt of thanks, Mrs. Dreyer.

"Thank *you*, agent Trupp, I appreciate everything you're doing for me," Sarah said as she stepped over to him and gave him a hug.

Sarah turned her head and watched as the medical examiner's men rolled the body of her father, wrapped in a gray plastic body bag, out of the house. She began to tear up again.

"I'd like to leave unless there's something else you need from me. I have a lot to do. I have to pick my daughters up from soccer camp at Tampa, and break the news to my mother. Then I have to come back here tomorrow and get this place ready for my mother."

"Sure, go ahead, your part in this investigation is over. Please, try and get some rest. You have another hard day ahead of you tomorrow," the detective told her.

"Thank you again for all your kindness," she told him as she hugged him again. She shook Guzman's hand and walked out the front door.

"Tell me something. Why did Harper come back to his house? What was so important? He didn't have any cash. No bank account information, nothing. Not even a piece of luggage," Guzman said.

"Who knows? Something got him here. Maybe there's something we missed in his briefcase. Whatever the reason, my guess is Herzog surprised him in the act and Vasquez came on the scene a few minutes later. Maybe we'll find something after we check out the rest of the house and his car. I know one thing for certain, Rich Herzog will be eternally grateful that Sarah Dreyer cared enough about her father to come by and check on him."

"You got that right. What a lady," Guzman said.

"I just wish she didn't have to come back tomorrow and deal with it all over again," Trupp lamented.

"She really doesn't have a choice about coming back tomorrow. Unfortunately, this is where the next chapter in her life begins."

"Yeah, I suppose you're right."

About the Author

Rick Stiens has been a business owner, soldier, coach & writer. Born and raised in Cincinnati, Ohio, Rick began working in the family business in the 6th grade, and continued working there through high school and college and returned there after serving in the Army.

He graduated from the University of Cincinnati with a Bachelors Degree in Political Science and has been a student of politics ever since. He has been published in a variety of local newspapers and has worked on various political campaigns.

Rick and his wife are living in south Florida, having moved from Cincinnati by way of Colorado. He has been a coach for all four of his children in a variety of sports. He has served on athletic boards, and community business groups in various locations.

His lifetime experiences have provided a wealth of opportunity to meet, work, and associate with people from all walks of life and locales. It is from this broad slice of life that he has drawn the composite characters for this manuscript.